Grave Decisions

Claire Highton-Stevenson

Copyright © 2019 Claire Highton-Stevenson
All rights reserved.
ISBN: 9781673960051

This is a work of fiction. Names, characters, businesses, places, events, locales, and incidents are either the products of the author's imagination or used in a fictitious manner. Any resemblance to actual persons, living or dead, or actual events is purely coincidental.

With thanks!

I am so thankful that you have made the decision to purchase this book. I hope that you enjoy it and will want to know more about me and my other books. If that is the case, why not join my mailing list? Not only will I keep you up to date on all my news and books, you will also get a copy of OUT: A Cam Thomas story for Free. You'll also be entered into a monthly draw for a free Signed copy of any book of mine, plus you'll get the chance to download free codes for audiobooks and a few short stories.

Subscribe right now and be in this month's draw! It's that simple: http://bit.ly/2D9BiXS

Dedication

My boys, Scouse, Elliot, Murphy, and Tumble, who thinks she's one of them!

Acknowledgements

Team ItsClaStevOffical
Nic, Frankie, Ann, Mari, Carmela
Elisabeth, Sandra, Judith, Carol
Sue, Pam, Kim, Miira, Kelly
Michelle Arnold – Editing
May Dawney – Cover design
My wife, my friends, my family

Prologue

It was hot, like a furnace. She could feel the cotton of her blouse sticking to her back as the sweat soaked into it. Her legs were numb from the cramped position she had been forced to lie in for the last hour – or more; she had lost track of time now. Her throat was dry. Screaming until she was hoarse had done nothing but parch her mouth. She licked at the slow drip of tears and sweat, her only source of liquid.

She squinted up as the sunlight poured in through the now-open boot.

"Please, just let me go." Her voice was croaky. She licked at dry lips. "I don't know what…"

He leaned in, lifting her with ease and slung her over his shoulder, ignoring her words. She had no fight in her. Drained and half-delirious, she flopped and banged against him rhythmically with every step he took as he marched away from the car, taking her somewhere.

To her death, no doubt.

She knew that. Somewhere in the back of her tired mind, she knew that this was it. This would be where her last breath would be drawn. For the last time, she thought about her kids, about Duncan, walking the dog.

The silence was eerie. But it wasn't silent, not if she really listened. Birds were whistling and there was a breeze, gentle but enough to sway the branches and rustle the leaves.

She landed in a heap on the ground. Her back hurt from something jagged and hard beneath her. When she tried to stand, her legs gave way, sending her crumpled back to the floor, looking up and into the face of the man she knew. He'd been nice then, smiled at her and talked about his own loss, his own issues. She had felt comfortable with him. He was dashing, wore an expensive suit, and helped people. It was why she had trusted him and stopped to help him.

Her only chance now was to run for it. She kicked off her shoes, and with a strength she didn't know she possessed, she raised herself up and sprang to her feet. Not daring to look back even for a second, she ran, her arms pumping up and down as her bare feet crunched against the dry earth. Her lungs burned with the effort, and then he was there, in front of her. She twisted away and moved in a different direction but he was too quick, cutting her off and charging after her. She turned, running back the way she had come, but he was faster, the crowbar cracking across her face as he stopped her in her tracks.

She fell to the floor, flailing and grabbing at nothing before she hit the deck. She groaned as she felt the blood dripping down her lip, salty and warm.

He bent down and easily picked her up, silently returning to where he had originally put her and dropping her down on the ground once more. Her head hit the ground and she felt a dizziness overcome her.

"Why?" she gasped out. Didn't she deserve to know why? He didn't speak. Instead his head turned to the left and she followed his gaze with her eyes. Four letters carved perfectly into white marble: Adam.

He pulled a half-bottle of vodka from his bag and held it out to her. "Drink!"

When she didn't take it, he grabbed her face and squeezed hard, her mouth opening reflexively as he poured the neat liquid down her throat. It burned, and she choked as it slid its way down like an inferno. Releasing her, he once more held out the bottle. "Drink it."

And now she understood. Now, everything made sense. Her hands shook as she reached for the bottle, clammy palms tightening around the cold glass.

He was her judge and jury.

He was her executioner.

Chapter One

The office was how it always was: comfortable. As usual, Sophie Whitton sat pensively and tried to calm her nerves. The soft furnishings felt itchy against her skin.

Her first appointment had been a few weeks ago and she had half expected an old woman in glasses wearing tweed. She had got the glasses part right, but Dr. Westbrook was far from old; she was in her forties and looked a decade younger. For the most part, she wore nice dresses with sensible cardigans, not a white coat. Sophie had mentally slapped herself for the assumptions; it wasn't like her to make them.

It was the Chief Inspector who had put her in touch with Dr. Westbrook. Whitton wasn't an idiot. The flashbacks weren't easing off; she wouldn't jeopardise a case by not being on top of her game. Slipping these sessions in was becoming routine, but leaving Dale to get on with things was the issue. He wasn't stupid either and would work it out eventually, if not ask her outright.

Dr. Westbrook waited patiently for the answer to her question. "I guess, I've never really given it much thought," Sophie finally replied.

The doctor half smiled. "You've never considered telling her?"

Sophie shook her head. "No, what would be the point?"

"Maybe it would help you if you shared what you're going through with her." It wasn't a question.

"That would be kind of selfish, wouldn't it!" That wasn't a question either, but Sophie knew she would get a reply, whether she wanted one or not. "Shouldn't I be capable of dealing with this myself? It's not like I don't deal with death every day."

"Sophie, Rachel almost died, that's a very important factor and something you are quite rightly upset about. Does she talk about it?"

"Not to me, no." She shrugged, "It's like everything else is perfect, and if we both just keep ignoring it, then it can't hurt us."

"Is that what you think it will do? Hurt you?"

Sophie remained silent, kicking herself for being caught out so easily. Of course it hurt her.

"Have you told her yet that you come here to see me?"

Whitton looked away, her sight drawn out of the window. It wasn't dark out yet, but with the light on in the office there was nothing to see outside, so she turned her attention back on the doctor. "No."

"When are you going to?" Her voice always remained calm, and it was one of the things Sophie liked when they talked. Even when she was shouting, Dr. Westbrook remained calm, pulling her back from the darkness.

"I wasn't planning to." Dr. Westbrook's brow raised as she waited for a further explanation. "If I tell her I see you, then she is going to ask why." There was the half smile again, and Sophie took up the challenge in it. "So, what? I go home tonight, ask her to come over, and then tell her that all I see when she isn't with me is her lifeless body, and would she be okay with moving in with me just so I can feel better, because I need to see her every day just to know she's alive."

"Is that what you want?"

Whitton's eyes narrowed. "Which part?"

"Do you want to see her every day?"

She ran her hand through her hair. It was growing longer; Rachel liked it like that. She liked to grab it and pull it when she came. "I want..." She toyed with the idea of telling her about the thoughts that went through her mind, but decided against it, fearful to acknowledge too much just yet. "I need to know she is safe."

"So, you don't want to live with her?" The question confused Sophie. She didn't know. Shouldn't she know by now?

"Not until I don't *need* to. I want to live with her because we're in love and it's the next step...not because I...because I am struggling to be normal." *Damn it*, she thought, kicking herself again. Westbrook would grab that "normal" and run with it.

The doctor sat back in her chair and placed her palms together as though she were about to say a prayer. "Why did she nearly die?" Her voice was so calm that it unnerved Whitton, and a waiting game of silence ensued, one that Dr. Westbrook would win. Whitton already knew that.

The armchair was suffocating. Whitton's scrawny frame felt confined within it, and she fidgeted, picking at the fluff on the navy trousers she had worn to work that day. There was a knot in her throat that made it hard to breathe properly. "Because I didn't get there in time," she finally stammered. "I wasn't good enough."

"That's not quite true though, is it?" Dr. Westbrook replied. "You and Dale did get there in time, didn't you? Because you left Rachel at home this morning, perfectly well."

Whitton nodded. "Yes."

"So, why did Rachel almost die?"

She swallowed and thought back to the man they had called The Doll Maker. "Because of Anthony."

"That's right, Rachel was hurt by Anthony, not by you. But it hurts you that she was hurt, because you love her." Dr. Westbrook's eyes softened, the half-smile becoming more pronounced. "And that would be the most *normal* reaction that a normal person could have."

Whitton almost laughed, thinking she had got away with the use of the word so flippantly. "When's it going to stop?"

"When you finally acknowledge that it wasn't your fault."

Chapter Two

DI Sophie Whitton stood back from the scene, smoking a cigarette. No onlookers, just the men and women in white Tyvek suits crowding around the corpse, taking notes, samples, photographs. The sun had dipped in the sky an hour ago, but it was still warm, especially under the floodlights that now lit up the area. Another balmy night lay ahead, a night of kicking off the duvet and wondering why she bothered to try and sleep anyway.

Finished with poisoning her lungs, she flicked the cigarette to the floor and stepped on it, grinding it into the sandy gravel until the last remnants of any flame were extinguished. Then she leant down and picked it up, pulled a plastic evidence bag from her pocket, and added the butt to the others she had smoked that weekend. Ignoring the growing bulge, she thrust the bag back into her pocket, pushed off from the car, and started walking.

The graveyard was immaculate. Clearly, the gardening staff took pride in keeping the place looking its best. In the distance, she could see someone on a ride-on lawnmower, turning back and forth as they cut the grass. Flowers bloomed, but on closer inspection, the grass was looking a little brown and patchy in places. The summer's sun was scorching its way across the Earth.

Her shirt stuck to her back as she moved. At least she had had the foresight to wear short sleeves, but still, the minute she got home to Rachel, she was heading for a cold shower to cool off.

Glancing around the scene, she took in the tranquillity of it: a church graveyard on the outskirts of Woodington. It was almost countryside this far out.

"St. Augustine's was built in 1810," Dale Saint's voice called out as he meandered back from taking a walk around the perimeter set up by Dr. Barnard's minions. "Nice, actually. All beautiful stained glass windows around the..." He stopped talking when she turned her head slowly to face him.

"Are those details going to help us catch this killer?" she asked in all seriousness, pulling her notepad from her pocket, ready to jot down the information. "Or do you think maybe time might be better spent finding clues?"

"No need for sarcasm." He grinned at her. They'd been partners on more occasions than he could remember. He was used to her and she him. "Wanna go and get a better look then, or just stand here sunbathing?"

He walked ahead, laughing to himself while she breathed deeply. In slowly, out slowly. *It's not her,* she told herself. *It's not her.* Several long strides and she had caught up with him.

"Nice place to end up," Dale said nonchalantly as he strolled alongside, keeping pace with her.

She gave him a withering look and shook her head. "Is it? Not something I really think much about, Dale." She swallowed the lie down. Who was she kidding? She thought about death all the time, just not her own.

"Yeah, well, I'm just saying, ya know, worse places you could end up."

"When I'm dead, I probably won't give a shit." Up ahead, the white overall-clad arm of Dr. Tristan Barnard rose up and waved at them. Even from this distance, he towered over everyone around him, a colossus of a man. His voice was already booming out orders.

"You don't give a shit now," Dale mumbled as he waved back at the giant up ahead. "But we all have to face it in the end." She ignored him, focusing only on putting one foot in front of the other.

"What have we got then, Doc?" she asked, still not making eye contact with anyone. The grave was a tidy one. Someone cared and looked after it at least, which was pretty much all you could expect and hope for once you'd passed on.

"Ah, Whitton. Nice of you to join us. Still sucking that toxic poison into your lungs, I see." If she was surprised that he had noticed her smoking, she didn't show it.

Instead, she pulled the sunglasses down her nose a little and glared at him. "Very observant. Anything else of any interest to offer?" She pushed the sunglasses back up her face and into place again. The body was still in situ, and she finally peered around him to get a better view. The woman was in her mid-forties maybe, brunette, business type, and if the ring on her finger was anything to go by, she was married. She was dressed in a simple grey skirt and white blouse; office attire. The thin material was ripped in places and covered in bits of dried-up old leaves and grass.

Whitton felt the air leave her body. Though she did her best to control it, she couldn't stop the heated flush that rose throughout her being. Her heart was beating so fast that she thought it might explode from her chest as dark hair morphed to blonde, the features changing to those of her girlfriend instead of the anonymous stranger.

"I would put time of death at four to six hours ago..." He flicked through the paperwork on his clipboard. "But, this here's the interesting thing." He grinned and squatted down, looking up at her, waiting for her attention. "See this?" He pointed down to where flesh was splintered with bone. "Broken post-mortem. Both legs."

She turned her head to face him, swallowing hard as the victim's face morphed into Rachel's again.

"What's the cause of death?" Whitton said, the flashback evaporating away as though it hadn't happened.

"Petechial hemorrhaging to the lower left palpebral conjunctiva and the bruising around the neck suggests manual strangulation at the very least rendered her unconscious." Barnard stood up and moved back to the woman's head. "I am going to stick my neck out and assume this finished her off," he said, lifting her head gently and pulling the hair away from her scalp to reveal a large bloodied gash. "My guess would be a hammer, a big hammer."

"Like a sledgehammer?" Dale asked, taking a better look. Whitton didn't move.

"Not quite that big, but something weighty."

"And then the killer placed her here and covered her with a sheet," Dale continued. He looked towards Whitton, whose face was still ashen, and his eyes narrowed at her. She shrugged it off and he let it go, much to her relief.

"Or he killed her here," Whitton suggested. Her mouth twisted to the side thoughtfully as she noted the information down in her book.

"I'd agree. The blood splatter and the amount of it would suggest she was alive until he, or she, brought her here," Barnard confirmed. The blood had congealed in a blackened pool around her head where she had bled.

"Anything personal on her?" Whitton continued, jotting everything down meticulously in her notebook.

"Just a credit card in her pocket and a locket around her neck. Photos of a man and two teenage girls. Her name is Anita Simmons." He picked up a clear forensics bag and held it up. The locket was open, and she could view two images. One side was indeed a man, around the same age as Anita. The other side held the image of two girls, not that much different in age, both with long red hair.

"So, you've confirmed her ID? How?"

"Detective, I know you know very well about my new toy." From a box by his feet, he pulled a small machine out. "Biometrics. Fingerprints scanned at the scene. She's in the system."

Now he had Whitton's attention. Her brows knitted together. "What for?"

"Come now, Whitton. Must I do all the work?" He winked at her.

Whitton felt the rush of air blow out from her cheeks as she glanced again at the victim, the dark hair blurring to blonde again. Her heart raced when she saw her lovers' green eyes staring back at her, lifeless.

"Why would anyone do that? It's overkill, right?" Dale looked down again at the body, laid out perfectly on top of the grave, his voice nudging Whitton back to the present. "It doesn't make sense," he said flatly when nothing else came to him.

Whitton turned to him. "It never makes sense." Turning back to Barnard, she asked, "What time's the post mortem?"

He turned his wrist, pulling back the elastic cuff to find his watch. "I suppose I could get it done tonight. Shall we say nine p.m. for the PM?" He chuckled at his play on words.

Whitton half-smiled before turning and walking away. She ducked under the police cordon and was set upon instantly by one of the local hacks.

"What can you tell us, is it another Doll Maker?"

"Fuck off," she snarled, already pulling her phone from her pocket. She found the number she needed at the top of her last-called list and sighed with relief the moment she heard the cheerful "Hello!" loud and clear through the handset.

"What? Come on Whitton, give us something to go on," the reporter continued to shout at her from his place behind the line, but she ignored him and concentrated on the call.

"Hey, I won't be home until later tonight, PM with Barnard at nine," she said, sucking in a breath and releasing it slowly. Rachel was fine, she was okay. "You still coming round?"

Rachel sighed. "Yes, I guess I will just have to entertain myself until you get here, won't I?" Sophie Whitton felt the flush of desire wrap her cells as her lover's voice dropped an octave and continued to inform her of the things she might do while she waited for Whitton to get home.

She turned away so that her words weren't carried on the breeze and into earshot. "So, you'll wait up for me then?"

"You know I will, Detective," her girlfriend purred seductively into her ear. She felt relieved that she would see her, lay hands on her, before the day was out.

Whitton hung up. Biting her lip, she let the arousal disperse before Dale noticed and made some corny, dirty little quip. He seemed to have grown some balls since the Doll Maker, a newfound confidence around her. She liked it, but she wouldn't encourage him by letting him know it. She owed him a debt. He'd saved Rachel.

Reaching the car, she held her palm out. "Keys?"

He dug into his pocket and tossed them to her while he pouted. "You know I *can* drive in both directions."

Smirking, she opened the door. "I know, and when you learn to put your foot down and get us where we need to be in a timelier fashion, I might consider letting you. Till then, buckle up, Buttercup."

He snorted. "One day I'm gonna report your blatant disregard for the speeding laws."

"Go for it." She half-smiled and pulled the car out of its parking space, increasing speed and turning into the road with barely a moment to stop and check for traffic. She noticed him stiffen and prepare for an impact. Of course, that wouldn't happen; she had already seen in her peripheral vision that the road was clear, but it was kind of fun to torment Dale when she could. "And then you'll be lumbered with some snotty-nosed arsehole that won't let you get away with half the stuff I do."

He grinned. "Fair point."

Chapter Three

Duncan Simmons looked defeated. He was sitting in an armchair, face ashen and staring off into space. His brown cardigan was not quite pulled around his shoulders right, as though he had dressed in a hurry that morning and not had time to straighten himself out.

"He's been like that since we told him," PC Watson explained in whispers. "He answers yes and no to questions, but pretty much in shock I think."

"You called a doctor in?" Whitton asked, her voice a whisper also.

"Family Liaison have organised it. They will be here as soon as they can." He shrugged. They both knew that resources were thin with FL and any doctor on call would be inundated already.

"Can you make us some tea? I need to speak to him."

Watson nodded and left the room.

Whitton looked around. The room was pretty big; they were doing well for themselves. The house was in an affluent part of town with a big drive out front that allowed for the two four by fours registered in their name. Only one was parked out front though.

"Mr. Simmons, my name is Detective Inspector Sophie Whitton. This is my colleague, DS Saint. We're sorry for your loss."

He glanced up at her, his eyes sweeping her face as though trying to find some kind of recognition, but he said nothing before returning his attention back towards the wall. Whitton followed his gaze. There was a framed photograph on the shelf of a middle-aged couple smiling at one another. They were dressed for a wedding or some other fancy celebration, champagne flutes in hand. To the outside world, this was a couple very much in love. That didn't always mean that it was true, and Whitton would keep an open mind like she did with everything. Many husbands had done the old woman in and then played the part of a shocked and devastated lover.

"Mr. Simmons, I wonder if you can tell me what Anita was supposed to be doing today? Where she was earlier? Where she was going?"

He said nothing. Dale raised his brows, his tongue pressed against the inside of his cheek, and then he blew out a breath,

"Did she work?"

Still nothing.

Whitton took a couple of steps and sat down on the sofa, leaning forward, elbows on her knees. "Mr. Simmons, I want to assure you that we are going to do all we can to find out what happened to your wife." His head turned at that and his eyes bore into her. "But, if I am going to do that, then I need you to help me, help her."

His jaw tightened; there was a rapid twitch in his cheek and his eyes filled with tears. "You people ruined her life," he hissed. "Trumped up charges, dragging her name through the mud. It was an accident and all you lot could do was try to ruin her."

Whitton let him get it out. He was angry, she understood that. His wife was dead and he needed someone to blame.

"No, she wasn't working. They sacked her and nobody else would touch her," he continued, his face reddening with anger.

Whitton kept her tone calm and continued the questions. "What did she used to do?"

He sighed, all the fight seeming to dissipate. "She was a..." He choked up and stammered the words out. "A s-social w-w-worker. She...she worked with kids and...and families, people in need." He rubbed at his face, smearing the tears across his cheek. "All she ever did was try and help people, and look how they treated her."

Watson appeared, carrying a tray with three mugs of strong tea. He placed it down on the coffee table and waited a beat to see if Whitton needed anything else. When she glanced up and nodded towards the door, he got the message and left quietly.

"So, the accident? Can you tell me what happened?" She moved one of the mugs towards him while Saint made a lunge for one for himself.

"Like you don't know," he sneered. "Made your minds up about her already."

"I can assure you, Mr. Simmons, my mind is open. I have only skimmed the basics. I'd like to hear your side."

It was hot in the room. The heat of summer was ramping up now that May was hurtling towards June. The heatwave would last a few more days, according to a multitude of weather reports across the TV networks that Rachel watched.

"They had a tough case. A sexual abuse case; it usually was." He shrugged. "Anyway, it had taken its toll on them all, and finally, they got the restraining order and the bloke was hauled off by you lot. But he got away with it." He reached for the cup and took a sip, wincing at the taste. "It's got sugar in it."

"It'll do you good," Saint said quietly. Duncan stared through him like he wasn't there.

Turning back to Whitton, he continued. "On the day they went to court, the team invited her to have a drink, commiserate, you know?" Whitton nodded and noticed Saint jotting it all down. "Next thing, I've got you lot banging down the door. On her way home she'd had an accident, a kid ran out in front of her and she couldn't stop. Hit him." He wiped his eyes again. "She did the right thing, called an ambulance. The police turned up and breathalysed her."

"It's standard procedure for anyone involved in an RTA," Whitton explained.

"Well, this machine was broken. Cos it came up with a false positive and she was arrested for driving under the influence." He laughed ironically. "She didn't drink!"

Whitton looked back towards the photograph. Two champagne flutes. Hers was half-empty. Saint followed her gaze, noted the same thing, and jotted it down.

"So, the kid? What happened to him?"

Duncan Simmons glared at her now. "He died."

Chapter Four

The murder board was wiped clean, just the 10 x 10 photograph of Anita Simmons stuck to the centre with four blobs of blue tac. Whitton held the dry marker in her left hand. She scribbled the name and DOB under the image. "Right, what do we know?"

Dale flipped open his notebook and read aloud. "Married to a Duncan Simmons of 4 Digna Place, Woodington. They have two kids, both girls. Cassandra and Josie."

He sat back and picked up his mug. Wincing at the almost cold brew, he put the cup back down and watched as Whitton continued to add the information to the boards.

"What was she arrested for?" Andy Bowen asked.

Dale tapped a few keys and brought up the report he'd already read. "Says she was involved in an RTA on Ashton Lane. Hit a kid called Adam Whitman. Killed instantly. Test said she was over the limit. Charged initially, but it seems there was a technicality and the CPS declined to take it further."

"When?"

"A year ago, almost to the day actually." He stood. Picking up his cup, he moved across the room to the kettle and flipped it on.

"The accident or the technicality?" Whitton asked, following the movement.

Saint looked up at her. "Both. Something to do with the machine that measured her initial breath test not being calibrated. By the time they took a second reading, she was below the limit and it was argued, successfully, that the original reading could have been similar, and therefore without a certificate to prove the machine was calibrated and in working order, it would be unfair to punish her." He shook his head. "Other than that, she has never been in trouble. Not even a parking ticket." He spooned coffee into two mugs.

Whitton read each board, moving onto the next and reading it carefully, then back to the previous, reading again. Saint watched. He was in awe of her most of the time, the way her brain connected the dots before most of them had even realised there was a dot to join.

"Coffee," he said, placing a mug down on the table. She turned briefly to acknowledge him before her attention was drawn back to the board in front of her. "We should get moving soon if we're going to the PM."

"Yeah," she said, glancing at her watch. One more look across the boards and she turned, picked up the mug, and took a sip. "I'll drink it on the way."

~Grave~

The pathologist's suite was still buzzing with activity even this late into the day. Forensic scientists worked just as hard as any other member of the judiciary. Whitton would forever be grateful for these people who worked tirelessly in order to bring them the evidence they needed to put the bad guys away.

It was a little past nine when she pushed the door open to Autopsy Room Four and entered. Barnard raised a hand and pointed to the microphone, indicating that it was on and he was recording his findings. He already had the Y incision done. The victim's organs were laid out tidily to the side, already examined, weighed, and recorded. He held what appeared to be her heart in his hand, ready to give his conclusions.

"...early signs of cardiomyopathy." Whitton raised a brow at Saint. Barnard continued on and recorded the details of weight on the chart before he switched off the microphone. "Detectives, nice of you to join us." He indicated the corpse.

"What have you got for us?" Whitton asked, ignoring his sarcasm.

Walking around the body, he stopped at the feet. "Well, this is interesting." He lifted the left foot. "As you can see, the victim has several abrasions, cuts, and marks on the soles of her feet, indicative of someone running or walking on rough terrain. There is also a lot of gravel and detritus embedded in the epidermis, but..." He held a finger in the air and placed the foot back down, picking up a crime scene photograph. "As you can see, she was found wearing her shoes. She also has a broken nose."

The shoes were now on the side table, wrapped in a clear plastic evidence bag alongside the victim's clothes, all waiting to be examined and processed. "So, she made a run for it and he punched her?"

Barnard shrugged. "Who knows if she made a run for it? The broken nose, however...I'm not sure it came from a punch. It's more a line across the bridge as though her face was hit with something like a thin bar? I can also confirm two fractured tibias and a fractured skull. All of her injuries, bar the head wound, occurred post-mortem but very quickly after death." He glided around the autopsy table once more and lifted the woman's brain, pointing out the large puncture mark. Whitton moved forward to take a closer look, while Saint found something else to look at. He looked a little green around the gills now they were in the morgue.

"Alcohol levels?"

Barnard nodded. "High; she would be considered over the limit."

"The husband said she doesn't drink," she interjected.

Exhaling, Barnard stiffened at the notion he might be wrong. "Well, she drank today. It will all be in my report."

"Not doubting you, Doc. Just thinking out loud," she said. Turning to Saint, she added, "Make a note to speak to the husband again, and track down the people she used to work with."

~Grave~

The office was empty when they got back near 11 p.m. Whitton flopped into her chair and woke the computer up. She input all the new information regarding Anita Simmons, listed the questions she had, and made a note of her early theories.

"You might as well knock off, Dale," she said across the desk to her partner.

"Yeah," he replied, stretching out his arms and yawning. "I guess it would be nice to see Becky for more than the few minutes as we pass each other in the mornings."

"Go, I won't be too far behind."

He grabbed his jacket and switched off the computer, patting himself down to make sure he hadn't forgotten anything. "Right, see you in the morning then."

"Night."

He hadn't been gone more than five minutes when the phone rang. She answered with a brusque, "Whitton."

"Ah, Detective Inspector, it's PC Carol Gardner. We've got a scene, we need someone from…"

"On my way, text me the details." She put the phone down and pulled her jacket from the back of the chair. Her phone beeped and she noted down the address. A pub in town.

Chapter Five

The town centre had bustled with what felt like half the population of Woodington earlier in the day. Maybe it was the summer sun and the unexpected heatwave that was slowly melting the tarmac drawing everyone into town, or maybe it was the newly laid square with its spouting fountains that entertained the kids. But whatever it was, it was busy. It was an opportunity for the beggars, who were lying about in shop doorways with their hands out to capture a few coppers in a polystyrene cup. There was less traffic on the road as people decided to walk to work rather than drive, and everyone seemed more likely to be polite.

Smiling children of all ages ran back and forth shrieking with delight, trying to dodge the meter-high stream of water that shot upwards in a random pattern while parents sat around on the concrete benches and caught up with one another over a takeaway coffee and a cigarette.

The sun seemed to bring out the best in people, but the heat brought out the worst in them. Now, as the night time air stilled and suffocated the daylight from existence, bars and pubs were full to bursting with everyone using the heat as an excuse to sneak a cheeky beer after work. The prospect of no work the next morning sent people on a bender of exuberance that often spilled over into chaos and carnage.

DI Sophie Whitton was now witnessing the aftermath of that from the periphery of the crime scene. The beer garden to the King's Head Pub in the centre of town was now empty of its usual clientele. Only the detritus of an abandoned night out remained in situ. And of course, Barnard's minions had made it past the tape, but it wasn't them that she was watching and listening to. With her eyes closed, she focused in on the sounds around her: the hushed voices of lab techs as they worked to comb the area for all the evidence on offer. The crowd surrounded her, people milling around wondering what had happened, others explaining the drama in all of its gory detail. She doubted any of them had actually witnessed anything, but uniform was all over it, interviewing everyone in the vicinity. She felt herself calm as she immersed herself in the environment.

Her head cocked to the right as she heard the loud baritone voice of Dr. Tristan Barnard cut through the cacophony, accompanied by the fluttering of the blue and white tape in the light summer breeze. She opened her eyes and searched him out. He was taller than everyone else by almost a foot; it wasn't difficult to find him as they exchanged glances and a simple nod of acknowledgement. He stood beside DC Jeff Branson, dwarfing the handsome detective.

It was humid, and the heat was still stifling. Not for the first time today was she grateful to be in short sleeves, but even that was doing little to stop the clammy night air from making her uncomfortable. The crime scene Tyvek coverall was only making things worse. She couldn't wait to finally get home and cool off with a cold shower.

A loud scream pulled her from her thoughts and she turned quickly to her left, just in time to catch sight of an overweight blonde woman being held back by an officer in uniform. Despite the heat, she wore a faux fur white leopard skin coat and a leather skirt that barely covered her backside as she launched herself at the PC, desperate to get past him. "Darren, Darren!" she screamed as tears dragged the remnants of mascara down her ruddy cheeks.

Whitton turned away from the scene. Lifting the blue and white taped police line, she ducked under and strode confidently towards the two men who would fill her in on all the details of this latest bloodshed.

"Detective Inspector Whitton, how lovely of you to join us again," Barnard said, a hint of mirth to his words as he looked up to see her stomping towards them. "Do you ever go home? I would have thought now that you—"

She cut him off. "What have we got then?" She jutted her chin towards the body lying prone on the ground. A pool of blood congealed around his groin and midriff. More blood was splattered around like a water hose had been let loose, but all she saw was

Rachel, lifeless and limp. Her heart broke a little every time. It sped up and threatened to explode as she tried to slow her breathing and not make a scene.

"Looks like a stabbing, Guv," DC Branson answered quickly, rubbing his chin. "Guv, you okay?" His soft brown eyes focused in on her, and she felt the light touch of his hand on her arm. Sound rushed back in and deafened her.

She turned towards the touch and shook herself, clearing her head of the image. "What?"

He studied her eyes, finding a silent plea to just let it go. She was grateful when he did. "According to witnesses, there was a fight. Two or three blokes getting rowdy over a spilled pint. Next thing, this guy was bleeding all over the place, and the others legged it."

She rolled her eyes at the waste of life over something so fucking trivial. "Right, do we have a name?" Her eyes were now firmly fixed on the body on the ground. *It's not Rachel, it's not Rachel,* the mantra in her head repeated.

"Wallet says Darren Barton."

Barnard nodded towards the technicians who would transport the body back to the lab. Whitton acknowledged Barry; she didn't know the other one's name. Barnard added, "I'll have more for you in the morning, but to be honest Whitton, it's a cut and dry stabbing. Quite simply, the femoral artery was severed and he bled out. But I'll have the official version with all the big fancy words on my desk by...shall we say 10 a.m.?"

The invitation to come along for a cup of tea and a formal discussion didn't go amiss with Whitton. "Sure, we will be there."

Chapter Six

It was just gone midnight when Whitton finally slid the key into the lock and pushed open the front door. She could hear music playing softly in the living room, the low hum of a Whitney Houston track. Shrugging off her jacket, she hung it on a hook and kicked off her shoes, breathing in the aroma of Rachel's perfume that lingered like a welcoming hug. She liked coming home to this. Having Rachel here when she got home made her feel at ease. The living room door was open, and light flooded the hallway. Rachel didn't like closed doors much now, not that Whitton could blame her.

Whitton felt the rush of air leave her lungs as she stepped inside and found the blonde nurse lying on her back on the sofa, her eyes closed. In an instant, she was transported back to the previous year and her worst nightmare.

She followed Dale into Rachel's cottage as they raced to get there in time. Her lover's lifeless body lay spread out on the couch, one arm flung limply to the side, hanging off the edge. Sophie's legs gave way, but Dale reached out and caught her, easing her to the ground before attending to Rachel.

She shook her head, gasping for breath as she gripped the back of the sofa.

"Hey." Rachel's sleepy voice broke through the fog. Her eyes were wide and alert. "I was just dozing off," she said, smiling up at her through sleepy eyes.

"Sorry, I just..." She ran a hand through her short, dark hair and licked her dry lips. Her heart rate beat rapidly still.

"Are you okay?" Rachel spoke softly as she stood and rounded the sofa. She gently placed her palms against Sophie's chest. When Sophie nodded unconvincingly, she asked, "What time is it?"

"Midnight, one? I dunno, I lost track. It's been hectic today." Rachel's lips pressed against the corner of Sophie's mouth before she finished speaking. She kept kissing her, her lips moving slowly and gently around the edge of Sophie's mouth, cheek, chin, always moving as Whitton began to join the chase.

"I can imagine. Wanna talk about it?" Rachel asked, her fingers deftly undoing each button until she could slide her palms inside the soft material, grazing gently over Sophie's skin.

Whitton shook her head, their noses brushing against one another. "No."

She sucked in a breath as Rachel cupped her naked breasts, fingertips gliding across her nipples. Finally, she let Whitton capture her lips, soft, so soft as they moved slowly against one another before parting to allow the probing intrusion of Sophie's tongue, sliding easily in contrast to one another, arousal building. "Hmm, shall I take your mind off of it?" Rachel murmured.

Nodding again, Whitton felt herself melting into Rachel's touch. Rachel had known how to play her from the very first moment they had met. Her touch always found a way to arouse her, take her mind away from the darkness. She found her eyes and held them, losing herself in the green. Rachel smiled, the corners of her eyes crinkling. She was so beautiful and *alive.* She needed to be reminded of that.

Rachel pulled at her shirt. Dragging it loose, she pushed it off to reveal bare, skinny shoulders. "You feel so tense," Rachel whispered before dropping slowly to her knees. She reached forward and unbuckled the skinny belt that held Whitton's trousers to her slender hips. Eyes locked and held as she worked the belt buckle loose and slid the zipper slowly downwards, smirking up at her lover. "I know just what you need." She smoldered under hooded eyes, and Sophie was sure she hadn't ever been more aroused than she was this very moment.

Rachel tugged the thin cotton material until it dropped with gravity and landed on the floor. The evidence of Sophie's desire trickled unhurriedly down her inner thigh until Rachel's tongue flicked out and licked slowly upward, meeting the line of Sophie's underwear. She heard the gentle hiss of anticipation from Sophie, felt the strong hand of her lover thread through her hair in expectation, and she liked it. She loved the way that Sophie's dominance so delicately straddled the line of erotic confidence. She peeled the shorts away and breathed in the spicy and powerful aroma of desire, enjoying the way that she could create such an abundance of wetness from her lover with just a few touches.

Sophie felt the muscles in her legs tense. Her glutes squeezed and relaxed as a rhythm began to build within her. Her hips pressed forwards, a hand tugging gently against Rachel's head, bringing her closer, moving her mouth nearer until she felt that familiar warmth overwhelm her senses. Rachel's lips, her mouth, and her tongue became the centre of Sophie's universe. Knowing, experienced and gentle lips sucked and kissed her intimately. Her hips began to thrust harder, her muscles tightening, and her stomach coiling and rolling.

It wouldn't take much, Sophie knew that. Rachel was too adept at this, too perceptive in her movements, knowing she would throw Whitton off her stride, forcing Sophie out to tumble over the edge. The two personalities of her lover were just as important, just as in control, but totally different. She loved nothing more than to start with Whitton and finish up with Sophie.

"Fuck, like that," Sophie moaned. Rachel smiled against her as the fingers in her hair tightened their grip. "Rachel...don't sto—" She didn't get to finish, the words lost somewhere in her throat.

~Grave~

Rachel arched, a stream of profanity leaving her lips as she tried clamping her trembling thighs around her lover's wrist, trapping her inside her as the orgasm Sophie had just evoked brought her shuddering to a wet, hot mess. A light sheen of sweat cooled her body, then she gasped for the breath she had been holding as her lover's fingers curled deep inside her again. "Fuck, you're so good at that." She smiled against Sophie's bare shoulder, nipping at the unblemished skin. The weight of her lover shifted to press against her, holding her legs apart. She gasped as Sophie's fingers continued to move, touching her deeply with firm, hard strokes that had her writhing again.

"Relax, let me take care of you," Sophie whispered, kissing her. The kiss moved from lips to neck and collarbone.

Rachel bit down on Sophie's shoulder. The insistent thrusting moved her against the sheets. Her hands gripped the cotton material, scrunching it between her fingers as her hips began to move, pressing up to meet every forceful thrust that Sophie offered until she could hold off no longer, gasping out a silent scream.

"Again," Whitton instructed, not giving her a chance to recover as this time she sped up her movements. Faster, harder. "Again," she urged. This time Whitton's kisses moved lower. Warm lips sucked at Rachel's nipple, licking and nipping at the soft skin of her breasts. Whitton followed the path down her torso, kissing the soft belly that she adored. Rachel gasped and groaned as Whitton withdrew her fingers and hooked her arms around her thighs, lifting her hips and taking her with her mouth, devouring her. She couldn't stop it. Whitton needed to feel her, needed to taste her and hold her. Her grip tightened around Rachel's hips, holding her tightly as she sealed her mouth to her, probing and lapping at her until Rachel was pleading and thrusting against her.

When Rachel stiffened, clamping her thighs together as she came again, and again, in an unmerciful explosion of pleasure that threatened to expose every raw nerve ending, she pleaded for her to stop. "No more."

"One more," Whitton insisted, gripping her hips more tightly.

Rachel pressed her palm against Whitton's head and pushed her away. "No, no more, babe...too much."

Whitton's loosened her grip and rested her head against Rachel's tummy, kissing the patch of skin there as she caught her breath, eyes screwed shut trying to work out what had just happened.

~Grave~

A summer rainstorm rattled the window. Raindrops splashed against the glass as Rachel rolled over and reached for a drink. "What brought that on?" she asked. Taking a sip, she let her tongue run across her dry lips, moistening them and tasting her lover again.

Whitton pushed herself up and leaned back against the headboard, the sheet draped across her legs. "I dunno, just…I needed to…" What did she need? Take her so many times just to prove she was alive? What if Rachel hadn't stopped her? What if she had just ignored her and…she felt sick at the thought.

Rachel swallowed down the water. "I'm not complaining. I love it when you get like that." She grinned and rolled back towards her. "You can take me like that anytime. I just want to make sure that you're okay."

Sophie nodded but avoided eye contact. "Yeah, I am now."

Twisting into Sophie, she snuggled against her side, slipping an arm around her waist. "I'm really happy, Soph."

"Good, would be pretty shitty if you weren't," she replied and wriggled when Rachel pinched her playfully. "I'm happy too."

"I was thinking that maybe soon we could...I dunno, share the same bed?"

"We are sharing the same bed," Sophie said, pursing her lips with one side twisting upwards into a half-smile.

Rachel leant on her elbow, resting her cheek in her palm. "Yeah, I think I'd just like to do it every night. I think I need to...like you need to know I am alive? I kind of need to know you're there."

Turning to face her, Sophie stroked her fingertips down her cheek, but she remained silent, just staring into the green that held her gaze.

"It's okay, it was just an idea."

"I'm not saying no...I just, let's keep talking about it, okay? It's a big decision, and if I am honest, one that I rushed with Yvonne." She leant in and kissed her chastely. "I don't want to rush anything with you. I love the way we are together; I love you."

"Do you?"

Whitton frowned and sat back. "Of course, don't you know that?"

"That's the first time you've said it." The gold in Rachel's eyes brightened as they flooded with unshed tears.

"I have said it, haven't I?" She was sure she had; she must have, because Rachel was the only light in her darkness. Rachel's presence in her life was everything now.

Rachel shook her head. "I didn't need you to until…until you just said it, and now, I realise how much I want to hear it."

"I'm so sorry. I'll do better," Sophie answered, pulling the curvaceous blonde towards her, her arms wrapping tightly around her. "I love you," she whispered again. "So much."

She lay awake in the dark as Rachel slept contentedly in her arms, not daring to move in case she disturbed the peaceful look on her face. Closing her own eyes just brought back images of her lover lying half-dead. She couldn't shake them, and she pushed the nausea back down, the darkness swallowing her up.

Chapter Seven

The morgue was busy again. Dr. Barnard's minions were buzzing about like annoying fly's in their navy blue scrubs and matching head coverings. Whitton's foot tapped rapidly as she sat in the uncomfortable plastic chair outside of Barnard's office. It was 11:03, and the pathologist was still finishing off the autopsy on Darren Barton. Dale had his head resting against the wall, eyes closed as he tried to grab a couple of minutes more sleep, grateful Whitton wasn't making them watch it.

Whitton yawned and then jumped up from her seat in order to pace the room. The autopsy results would be pretty cut and dry. All she needed was a rundown from the doc and they could get on with tracking the guy that pulled the knife. She already had other officers on the CCTV, tracking the moron's every move. If she was lucky, they'd have it all wrapped up by the end of the day. She stretched and felt her spine crack back into place.

"Huh? What?" Dale jumped and sat up instantly.

Whitton faced him. "Rough night?"

He moved his neck left and right as he yawned. "Yeah, Harry has a cough."

Whitton nodded; his youngest daughter was a sweetheart usually. "Well, try and keep awake for the important things and maybe we can knock off early."

"That would be pretty good." He looked around the room and then glanced down at his watch. "Doc's late, ain't he?"

Whitton rolled her eyes at him, but she checked her watch anyway. He wasn't that late, and she would wait anyway.

"Ah, detectives." The man in question's voice boomed as he came into the room, taking up all of the space in the doorway. His tall stature was equal to his build. "So sorry for keeping you waiting…" He looked from one to the other, a mixture of mirth and glee on his features. "You're here for the Barton case, correct?"

Whitton nodded. "Yes, sir."

"Hmm well, yes, yes, yes, that's all as we thought. Single stab wound to the upper left thigh that nicked the femoral artery, causing death within a few short minutes." He handed over a file and Whitton took it. She studied him for a moment and noted the other file still in his grasp. "I'd say that you're looking for a small knife. 3-inch blade at most."

"What else?" she asked.

"Oh, Detective, you know me so well. Have a seat. Tea?" he asked, placing the file down on his desk. He crossed the room in just three steps. Lifting the kettle, he shook it to judge the amount of water it held and then, satisfied, placed it back down on the base and flicked the switch that would have it boil. He turned back to face them both, holding two china mugs in his hand as an indication.

"No, thank you," she said. Dale Saint nodded yes and followed his boss in taking a seat on the antique couch.

While the doctor fussed with his teapot, he continued on. "Anita Simmons," he stated so they understood he had moved on from the pub fight. "Her clothes were soaked with alcohol. Particularly around the front part of her blouse and her lap."

He watched with interest as Whitton worked it out. "She was forced to drink it?"

~Grave~

Smoke wafted up into the air as Whitton blew out. She waited for Dale to catch up. It was another sweltering day, and she was at least thankful that she had been inside the air-conditioned building. Now though, the heat hit hard. An ambulance screeched past with its lights flashing. An eerie silence following when the siren had been cut off.

"I need a coffee before we do anything else," she said, walking off towards the main building.

"When are you going to tell him that you don't like that shit tea he serves?" Dale laughed.

"When he stops looking at me like I am his favourite detective." She grinned back, aware that Dr. Tristan Barnard had a little crush on her. It didn't hurt to use that knowledge for leverage now and then.

Woodington General Hospital was the best and nearest place to get a decent caffeine hit. They waited in line like everyone else. "Think this heat is here for the duration?" Dale asked, fanning himself with a packaged chicken mayo sandwich.

"I think Rachel said something about a heatwave lasting several weeks."

"Fuck. I dunno how much more I can take."

She looked down the queue to see how much longer they had to wait. Three people ahead of them. "Well, I'll put a word in with the guv and see if he might go for paddling pools in the office," she deadpanned.

"Har har." He shoved his sandwich at her. "Get me a large coffee, I need to take a piss."

Her eyebrow raised, but she took the sandwich and nodded. Just two now in front of her. Placing Dale's choice of sandwich down onto the tray, she slid it along and reached over for a blueberry muffin.

A voice in her ear whispered, "Hello, Detective." A shot of arousal hit her and she felt the tension instantly leave her body.

"Nurse," she replied sternly without looking back, as the body behind pushed up against her. She relished the feeling she got from it.

"What are you doing here?" Rachel asked as she slipped in front of Whitton in the queue. Her eyes locked and held Whitton's gaze in place. Dark green with flecks of gold shone at her in a teasing manner that Whitton was still getting used to.

"Same as you, getting coffee."

Rachel grinned at the remark. "God, I need it, too. This heat seems to bring out the worst in people. Three fights resulting in a stabbing already this morning. The surgeons are whining like bitches about it." She grinned and reached across Sophie to grab an apple, placing it alongside Dale's sandwich on the tray.

Sophie Whitton pushed her tray along as the last person in front of her finished paying and moved on. She ordered three coffees and readied to pay the elderly woman on the till; her name badge read Gladys and said that she was a volunteer. Whitton smiled at her and got a half-hearted grin in return.

"Are you joining us?" Sophie asked Rachel as she caught sight of Dale approaching out of the corner of her eye. She handed over a ten-pound note and waited for her change with her hand out as she turned back to face Rachel.

"No, I need to get back. But I'll see you tonight, right?" She grabbed the apple and took a cup of coffee.

"Maybe..." Sophie teased.

Rachel licked her lips. Capturing the bottom one between her teeth, she grinned. "Oh, there will be no maybe about it, Detective." And with a wink, she turned and walked away, the sway of her hips very much in Whitton's line of sight.

Whitton plonked the tray down on the nearest free table, narrowly avoiding spilling either coffee. The liquid ebbed and flowed across the expanse of the cups but only licked at the edges. One by one she took the items from the tray and placed them down on the table. She then filled the tray with the dirty plates and packaging from the last resident of the seating area; people were just so lazy. Twisting around, she saw the metal cage that housed trays with dirty dishes and took hers to it. Sliding it into the space, she wiped her hands down her trouser legs and stalked back to her seat. Dale was now sitting opposite, his sandwich already unwrapped and a large bite missing from one half.

"So, what d'ya think?" he asked, a mouthful of food churning like a tumble dryer.

"Dunno." She shrugged and brushed her hand through her short hair, pushing the long fringe from her face. "It all just feels...off."

He swallowed down the last of his sandwich and took a mouthful of coffee. "I thought moving here would mean a quieter life. Somewhere safe to bring the girls up. Instead it's like Serial Killer City."

Whitton grinned. "You should copyright that and sell it to the hacks at the Chronicle." She tossed the remainder of her muffin down on the plate. "You ready? Let's go talk to this Diane Boyce."

Chapter Eight

Diane Boyce lived at Number 12 Manchester Gardens. Her home was immaculate. Even as Whitton walked up the path, closing the soft-shut gate behind her, she could tell this was going to be a home with nothing out of place. The small patch of grass was manicured to within an inch of its life. Perfect edges and weed-free borders lined a swept and mopped tiled pathway to the door.

The door opened without either of them having to knock. A short woman with greying hair, dressed in a housecoat, smiled at them. Whitton wasn't sure the last time she had seen anyone wearing a housecoat, and she was pretty sure that Saint wouldn't even know what one was.

After introductions had been made, Saint and Whitton were invited in. With the kettle boiling and Mrs. Boyce otherwise engaged with making the pot of tea (because it would be a *pot* of tea, that much Whitton was certain of; Mrs. Boyce didn't strike her as the one-cup teabag kind of woman), Saint took a seat on the plastic-covered sofa and winced as he almost slid right off. Whitton stifled a laugh and took the opportunity to look around. Shelving behind glass cabinet doors housed lots of miniature china ornaments. Not a spot of dust anywhere. The walls were dotted with photographs of loved ones. Everything had a place.

"Here we go." The joyful voice of Mrs. Boyce rang out before she had even entered the room. Her cheery face soon caught up though, and a tray with three cups and saucers, plus a china pot, came into view. "Tea for three."

"Thank you, Mrs. Boyce," Dale said as he carefully slid forward to help her settle the tray down on the coffee table. *Ironic,* thought Whitton. Why were they never called tea tables?

"One for you. DI Whitton, did you say?"

She turned and smiled slowly at the mention of her name, taking the cup and saucer offered. "Yes, that's right."

Mrs. Boyce pointed to the plastic-covered armchair and indicated that she should sit there. Whitton glanced at Dale, his brow raised in mirth as he waited for her to understand just how slippery it was. She squatted slowly and perched on the edge as best she could without falling off, grateful for a strong core of musculature that kept her in place.

"What can you tell us about Anita Simmons?" she asked as the older woman found a spot next to Dale. Clearly, it was her spot. The seat, though perfectly new underneath the plastic, had a slight indentation in the padding where someone obviously sat frequently.

"She was a nice woman, did her best; we all did…but I think…" She stopped speaking and placed her cup down. "I don't like to speak ill of the dead. I still can't believe she is, to be honest; she was making such progress."

"Mrs. Boyce, anything you can tell us, it might seem insignificant, but it could help us work out what happened to Anita," Whitton said softly, always knowing the right tact to take with witnesses.

Diane exhaled loudly. "Anita joined our team, oh, maybe 13 or 14 years ago. She fit right in; kindness ran through that woman's heart. But it wears you down, that kind of work. The things you see and hear – it's shocking what humans can do to one another in the name of love."

Whitton smiled and nodded. She understood that all too well.

"Obviously, you know what I mean. The things you both must see." She shook her head and visibly shivered. "We all liked to unwind, sometimes after work, mostly at the weekend. A drink here and there to talk about the day, decompress I think they call it." She smiled at the memory. "Anita…she seemed to decompress a little more than the rest of us. After-work drinks turned to a quick tipple at lunch and well, several of us saw…in her bag, those little bottles of spirits?" She made out the size with her fingers.

"So, she *was* drinking at work?" Dale asked, to be clear and to write the answer in his book. Diane Boyce nodded.

"Yes, it all came to a head one afternoon when a victim we were working with killed herself. We'd taken her abuser to court, but the court had thrown it out; lack of evidence. Anita took it hard, she felt like she had let the woman down. That was the day that she drove home and…well, I am sure you know what happened." She shook her head. "That poor boy."

Dale placed his cup back down on the saucer. "In your opinion, Anita had been drinking that day?"

"I can't say for sure."

"What happened next?" Whitton asked before taking a sip of tea.

"Well, she was suspended from work obviously. She had been arrested and charged. There was an investigation, and to be honest, I thought it was a little unfair."

"In what way?"

"They investigated and made a decision before the trial had even begun. She was sacked without ever being found guilty of anything. In my opinion, she needed help."

"Did you ever speak to her after she left?"

Diane nodded. "Yes, often. We would have coffee together maybe once a month. I remember being really pleased for her that she was getting help. She confided in me that she hadn't touched a drop since the accident. She swore that she wasn't drunk, she had had one small vodka before she left, but that wouldn't have been enough to impair her driving or to have failed the breath test."

"So, getting off on a technicality was a blessing for her then?"

"I suppose so. She was remorseful, Detective. Not a day went by when she didn't think of that poor boy. She even started working at the help group she attended. She said she wanted to help others come to terms with the things that upset them and turned them to drink or other self-destructive coping methods."

Whitton sipped her tea. "Did she speak about her husband? Duncan?"

"Often." She smiled again. "She loved that man. Said he was her rock."

The DI frowned. "And yet, he doesn't know about her drink problem."

"That wouldn't surprise me. Anita wasn't proud of it, she hid it from us as best she could. It was easier to hide it from Duncan and the girls, and it wasn't like she was a real drinker, just the odd one or two here and there."

Whitton placed her cup down, half a cup of tea still swilling around. "Well, thank you for your help." She stood, and Dale followed suit. "Oh, just one thing…do you know where the self-help group was?"

"Yes, it's called Mute Air, or something like that. A woman named Jewel runs it, strange names if you ask me." She smiled a warm, gentle smile.

"Mute Air? Okay, thanks very much."

Outside, Whitton pulled the keys from her pocket. "Let's get back to the office and find out what we can about this place, then I wanna take a visit."

Chapter Nine

A fan had appeared in the office Monday morning. It gently whirred left and right, circulating stale, warm air around the room. Mugs with dregs of cold coffee were now strategically placed on desks, holding paperwork down.

"Mutare!" Saint read from the website he had found. "It means 'change' in Latin." He scribbled the word and its meaning down on a notepad. Rubbing his face with his hands, he yawned as he twisted the pad around to show Whitton.

"What else does it say?" she asked, peering over his shoulder to look at the website. His aftershave was light and fruity. She wondered how Becky had finally convinced him to change. It was certainly a better option than the overpowering men's spray he had used in the past.

Deft fingertips moved the mouse around the screen until it hit the word *About,* and then he clicked and opened up the page.

"Here at Mutare, we hope to bring a change to your life. With our guidance, we can lead you through the darkness and bring you everlasting peace.

A new way forward.

Are you ready to stop hurting yourself?

Let Jewel and Galahad show you the way.

Call in for change, Mutare is the only way."

"Galahad? That's got to be made up, right?" Dale asked, a tone of disbelief wrapped up in a chuckle.

Whitton raised a brow and smirked. She straightened up and stretched out her spine.

"Mu-tar-re," Saint repeated in his best Italian accent. He leant back in his chair triumphantly and grinned up at her.

"You ever been to Italy?" She turned and perched on the corner of his desk.

"Spent two weeks in Sorrento with Becky before the kids were born. Was very nice. You should take Rachel. Very romantic as I recall."

She grimaced at him. "I'd rather you didn't recall anything about romantic times with Becky, thank you." She smirked at him again and pushed off from his desk. "Gimme ten minutes. We can go and take a look around Mu-tar-re."

~Grave~

The address given on the website for Mutare was a small semi-detached ex-council house near the centre of Woodington. Nothing about it stood out, apart from the two disheveled-looking men standing outside on the street. Beside them a nervous-looking woman in a business suit fidgeted about, checking her watch every twenty seconds. Whitton looked around at the house next door. A curtain twitched back into place, the observer no longer observing quite so obviously.

Whitton turned her attention back to the building that housed Mutare. The garden was much like the first two men in the queue outside, a little unkempt and untidy. The small patch of grass was uncut and full of wildflowers, or weeds; she didn't know the difference. It didn't look like it had had a trim all summer. Two rose bushes and an abundance of more obvious weeds lined the path. Some of the weeds were quite nice, beautiful flowers hanging off them as they pushed through the unwanted plants around it, the ones that would suffocate and kill anything that got in their way. It was the green bin that caught Whitton's eye next. Someone had cello-taped a laminated sign on the front of it.

Take the first step.

Leave the crutches of life behind.

Whitton lifted the lid and peered inside; the stench was unreal. Empty vodka bottles filled most of the space, with the odd medicine bottle or pill packaging poked out from between. But where bottles had smashed against one another and broken, any liquid left had mixed to create a potent stench of alcoholic punch. "Jesus, that's rank."

Saint wafted away the stink with his hand. "I bet the neighbours ain't too pleased with this," he stated, his line of sight on the window where the curtain-twitcher had been. He tugged at his shirt, pulling it back and forth in an effort to cool his skin. There was no letup from the summer heat, which would only exacerbate the concoction boiling away in the bin like a rancid chemistry lesson.

"Would you be?" she scoffed, knowing full well he wouldn't. She dropped the lid shut again. "Come on, let's check it out."

They wandered up to the gate. The two men paid barely any attention to them, disinterested, but the woman stared wide-eyed and checked her watch again. The action caused Whitton to do the same. Two minutes to one.

"They don't open till one." The deep voice of one of the men came from behind her. She swiveled on her heel, searching him out with her eyes. Tall and lanky, he held her gaze with confidence.

"Right, thanks."

"First time?" he asked. She pulled her cigarettes from her pocket and opened the pack. His eyes moved towards them swiftly and lingered. Pulling one out, she lit it and took a deep pull on it.

"Yes, first time." She held the packet towards him and he reached out. Shaking fingers picked one and slid it out. She offered the pack to the other man, but he shook his head.

"No thanks, one addiction's enough for me." He grinned, and she noticed his lack of front teeth. The first man leant forwards towards her lighter and sucked in a toxic breath just as she had.

"So, what's it like?" she asked nonchalantly as they smoked.

The first man looked back at the house, his hand shaking as he brought the cigarette to his lips once more. "It's alright, better than some of the other groups I've tried." He leant in casually and spoke in a lower tone. "She's a little cuckoo if you ask me." He winked and grinned as he stepped back and took another pull. "But, most of what she says hits home. She doesn't hold back, and if ya think you're going to get an easy ride…well, think on. I'm Jim, by the way."

"Right. Actually, I'm not here for the program." Jim's hand stopped halfway to his mouth. His eyes were fixed on her, and the muscle in his cheek twitched as he considered what that meant. She reached into her pocket and pulled out her warrant card, holding it up for him to see.

"Go on."

"Anita Simmons? What can you tell me about her?"

"Not much, kept herself to herself. Very kind and helpful is Anita. If you need information or help with anything on the computer and stuff, she's the one to ask."

"What about you?" Whitton said, turning now to face the nervous woman.

"Me?" She raised a manicured nail and pointed to herself. Whitton nodded and kept her eyes on the woman. She fidgeted about and checked her watch again. "I don't know her. I mean, I've seen her…here, but I don't know her."

"Okay, and what is your impression of her?"

"I don't know, she's like the rest of…" She looked around before lowering her voice. "She's like all of us. On the wrong path and looking for an answer."

Whitton appreciated the candour. She lowered her own voice and stepped forward. "So, you're here for the program too?"

The woman nodded. "Yes," she whispered. "It's my lunch break, I try and fit a class in as often as I can."

The woman didn't look like an addict, not in the stereotypical sense, but Whitton knew from experience that that wasn't always the way addicts presented. "It's helping?"

"Yes, I haven't had a drink for over six months. Not since I threw the bottle I kept in my bag into that bin," she answered, pointing towards the bin. "That's why I remember her. She said she had been the same. Secret drinking, you know?"

Saint jotted the information down.

"Anita was found dead Friday afternoon," Whitton announced loudly enough for all to hear.

Two more men had joined the queue. Movement from the left indicated that the doors were now open as Jim and his friend moved off from the gate and started up the garden path.

"I'm sorry I can't help Officer, I have to go." She checked her watch again. "Important meeting later and I can't be late, or miss this one."

Dale Saint leaned against the car, just watching. Whitton joined him and both of them took notice of the people who arrived and left over the next hour. Those that left appeared to give them a wide berth, eyes either avoiding contact altogether, or openly glaring at them.

"I'd say we've made our presence known," Dale said, nudging her with his elbow, chin jutting back towards the curtain twitcher.

"Yeah." She opened the door. "Drop me off in town. Then pick me up from home around six. We can come back here and see what this Jewel has to say."

Chapter Ten

The lights were on inside the home that housed Mutare. It was darker now, but still light enough to see up and down the street. The curtain twitched next door, but it was pretty quiet on the whole.

"Come on, let me lead you up the garden path." Dale snickered. Opening the gate, he held it open for Whitton as she rolled her eyes at him. Each window had a blind drawn, the light of the room creeping out from around the edges. There was music coming from inside – not loud, but audible as they got closer. A gentle swishing of waves and rainfall intermixed with a soft panpipe that was clearly indicative of meditation. "Got ya zen ready?"

"You should try a bit of meditation, Dale. Might make you more at one with your fellow man, or woman."

"I dunno what you mean." He grinned as his finger pressed the doorbell.

The door opened moments later. The unamused face of Jewel Benson stared back at them. "What now!" she huffed belligerently. "We are trying to save them, and it really doesn't help being interrupted like this during the essential flow of the existential universe."

"Yeah, I am sorry about that. Maybe we can wait somewhere until you're done?" Whitton suggested as she stepped forward and over the threshold, her palm pushing the door open a little wider. She could see a room to the left. The door was ajar, and the soft music they could hear from outside was now louder and clearer; meditation music for sure. Several bewildered faces stared at them.

Jewel looked a little unsettled, flustered even at their presence, but she nodded and stepped aside. "Just don't *touch* anything," she demanded as she led the way towards a room opposite the meditation. "I don't want your imprint. My things are cleansed and free from the negativity that people like you carry."

Dale shifted uncomfortably behind Sophie. "I think we can manage that," Whitton said, her face unreadable as she stepped forward once again and entered the room. The door closed behind them with a bang.

"She's something else. People like us?" Dale grumbled. "Can we just arrest her for the fun of it? I am sure we can find some reason to lock her up for a night."

"Obnoxiousness isn't a crime, sadly," Whitton answered, her back to him still as she perused the room. It was a living room, of sorts. Large cushions were on the floor instead of sofas. A low coffee table made of dark wood sat in the middle of the room, the top covered with an inlay of porcelain decorative tiles depicting a scene of fairies and pixies that floated around a garden of exotic plants. Salt lamps and lava lamps dotted around on the surfaces of dark wooden shelving, interspersed with crystals of all shapes and sizes.

Saint sniffed. "It stinks in here," he complained. Whitton reached down and picked up a long, flat box and waved it at him.

"Incense, I presume."

"Well, I am incensed by it." He grinned as Whitton placed the box back where she found it. "And you're not supposed to touch."

She raised a brow and lightly touched the nearest object to her. "Is that so?"

The music from across the hall came to a halt. Muffled voices and shuffling of shoes alerted both officers to the fact that people were leaving. Whitton checked her watch. They'd been waiting just over 15 minutes. She heard Dale mutter that it was about time, and then the door swung open.

Jewel entered, her kaftan flowing around her as she sauntered back into the room. She held her head high and stood there, poised and composed. "Well, I am sure you're aware of just how much your negativity has soured the ambiance of this evening," she stated. Saint looked to Whitton, who shrugged.

"We wanted to ask you a few questions." She noticed the eye roll and sagging shoulders, like a petulant teenager. Whitton reached into her inside pocket and produced a colour photo taken of the deceased woman at the morgue. "Anita Simmons?"

Jewel huffed but took a step forward. Reaching for the photo, she took it between two fingers as though it were contaminated. Handing it back, she shook her head.

Whitton held it up in front of her and snarled, "Try actually looking at it."

Jewel cut her eyes at Whitton. "I don't need to look at a photograph to tell you that I knew Anita." Whitton thought for a moment that she detected some actual sorrow towards the woman. "I can't believe that she isn't with us any longer. I don't know how to open any of the files she organised on the computer. It's really messed everything up, I'm all over the place," she whined.

"Yes, I can imagine her dying on you like that must be inconvenient." Sarcasm dripped from Whitton like a melted candle, all of it lost on the woman.

"Yes," she sighed and ran her hand through her hair.

"What can you tell me about her?"

"Hold on." Jewel held a finger up as she thought. "Wait a minute." With that, she turned and dashed out of the room. Whitton raised an eyebrow at Saint, who shrugged in return. They could hear the woman mumbling to herself as she wandered back into the room holding a piece of paper in her hand. "Anita Simmons, that's the official information I have."

"She came here for how long?"

Jewel shook her head and shrugged. "I don't know, it's in there." She pointed at the piece of paper. "Thank goodness we kept the old records."

"Guess," Dale said, ignoring her selfish grumblings.

"Six months?"

"Six months? Is that all?"

She rolled her eyes at him and hissed. "Yes, are you calling me a liar?"

"Not at all."

"Well, they might lie to you, but they know that I am here to help them and as such..." Her face reddened and she pursed her lips in anger at him.

"Okay, okay," Whitton said, her palms up. "Anita came here for what reason?

Jewel Benson moved her gaze from Saint and back to Whitton. "Initially she said she wanted to stop drinking. It had become a habit to take a secret drink and she was scared that it might get worse after the…accident. So, we worked with her on that and after a while, she began to mentor some of our other clients." She sighed. "She was very good with them, especially the younger ones."

"Is it possible that she was still drinking?"

"What are you getting at?" Her face scrunched as she contemplated the question. "No, definitely not. She had come to terms with everything that happened. She understood that Constance Martin's death wasn't her fault."

Whitton's gaze intensified. "She talked about Ms. Martin? Her client?"

"Of course, it's part of the therapy. To discuss, explain, and understand your circumstances. Anita was very open to it. It was Connie who told her about us."

"Constance came here too?"

"Yes, for support."

"She didn't want to see a professional?" Dale asked, a hint of snide in his voice.

"I don't like your tone. These people come here for help, and we give it to them. Anita was doing fine, we—"

"We?"

The woman hesitated before answering. "Yes, my husband and I, we were very proud of her."

"Ah yes, Galahad, right? Where is he? Can we speak with him?" Whitton asked, looking over the woman's shoulder towards the partially open door.

Jewel stiffened. It was almost imperceptible, but Whitton noticed it. "He isn't here right now. So, no."

"Where is he?"

"Away...he is on a business trip." She shuffled from side to side. The piece of paper in her hand rustled as she moved it from one hand to the other.

"Right, well I want to talk to him. So, make sure that he calls me the moment he is back in town." Whitton reached into her pocket and pulled out a business card with her number on it. "The minute he is back in town," she reiterated before looking at Dale and nodding her head towards the door to indicate they were leaving.

~Grave~

Outside, she pulled her cigarettes from her pocket and lit one. Dale loosened his tie. "Is it me or does she give off an air of not quite all there?" They were standing by the car, so he leant against it. Darker skies were moving in, another sultry night in store for them all.

Nodding in agreement, Whitton took a long drag and blew the white smoke up and into the air; the only cloud in view.

"I don't like her."

"Not so sure she likes you much either," Whitton deadpanned before smirking at him and continuing to smoke. "You wanna drive?" She tossed the keys at him. Grinning, Saint hit the fob buttons for the car alarm and opened the door, fanning himself as the heat escaped. Whitton finished her cigarette and opened the passenger door, climbing in in unison with Saint. He turned the engine over and then fiddled with the aircon until he had a warm breeze blowing out from the vents. It didn't take long for cooler air to start coming through.

"Thank you, aircon!" He fist-pumped the air and smacked the steering wheel. "Back to base then?" he asked, turning towards Whitton. She was focused on a message on her phone.

"Nah, drop me home then get off, we can pick up again in the morning."

Chapter Eleven

"What do you want me to do?" asked Jeff Branson. He had gained a reputation for two things since joining the team: his genius with computers and CCTV, and being the team hunk. He looked like Idris Elba's twin brother, only a decade younger.

"Start with Anita and work backwards. See if you can spot anything suspicious on any of the CCTV that she would have come into contact with. The chances of there still being anything much we can find in the other two is slim, but if anyone is going to find it, it's you," Whitton praised, and he grinned back at her.

"You know it. If it's there, I will find it."

"What are we doing?" Dale asked, eager to get stuck into something. She didn't reply. Instead she unpinned the photograph of Anita Simmons' body lying serenely on top of the grave.

"Fuck," she muttered. "How did I miss that?" A flash of Rachel's face told her exactly why she had missed it; her mind wasn't focusing. She was losing her touch.

"What? What is it?" Dale said, moving the short space from his desk to where she stood. She handed him the picture and pointed at the grave's headstone.

It was white marble, pristine and carved perfectly with small letters that read:

Here lies

Adam Michael Whitman

Taken too soon into the arms of our Lord.

2006-2018

"We're going to speak to the parents of Adam Whitman," Whitton said, striding away.

~Grave~

Farmland wasn't somewhere Whitton had ventured much in her life so far. Judging by the mud and the smell, it wasn't somewhere she planned to visit again if she could avoid it. Her boots were already caked, and the stench of animals' manure reeked. This kind of summer heat was doing nothing to lessen its impact on her nasal cavities.

"Jesus, who the fuck can live with this?" she asked Saint as they both walked towards the only building that looked like a house.

"Becky reckons having a small holding would be the perfect retirement," he answered, scrunching up his nose. "Not a fucking chance!"

"Somehow I don't see you in a flat cap and wellies." She smirked at him and almost slipped in a patch of mud.

The house was a little rundown. Windows needed repainting, and the door looked as though it was the original and dated 200 years. The distant growl of a tractor somewhere to the left, at the back of a field, drew their attention for a moment. When they looked back, the front door was open and a short, stout woman in navy overalls stood wiping her hands on an oily rag. "Are you lost?"

"Uh, no," Whitton said, treading carefully until she reached the makings of what she thought might be a path. "We wanted to speak to Mr. & Mrs. Whitman. DI Whitton and DS Saint." She held out her warrant card. The woman's face drained.

"What's happened? Is my Kenny alright?"

"Yes, sorry, I don't know who Kenny is. We just have some questions we thought you might be able to help with."

The woman looked them up and down, as though she were making a decision, colour returning to her cheeks. "You'd best come in then." Eyeing their shoes, she added, "You can leave those outside."

~Grave~

There was no offer of tea. No welcome or invitation to sit. Audrey Whitman shoved the rag into her pocket and got straight to it.

"What do you want?"

Whitton considered how best to broach the subject. There was no easy way to bring up the death of a child with a grieving parent. "We are investigating the murder of Anita Simmons."

The woman's eyes widened. "She's dead? Someone killed her?"

Whitton nodded. "Yes, and then they placed her body on Adam's grave."

The ashen, pinched features now turned beet red as anger came to the fore. "They did what? Why would they do that?"

"We don't know. Right now, we are investigating every lead and…"

"You think we had something to do with it?"

Shaking her head, Whitton stepped forward. "What we know is that Anita Simmons was forced to swallow vodka and then killed. She was then placed, as I said, on top of Adam's grave."

"And you want to know if we had anything to do with it?"

"It's a line of inquiry that we are duty-bound to investigate," Whitton said. "I don't think that's the case, but we would be negligent if we didn't ask the questions."

"When?"

"I don't…"

"When was she murdered?"

"Friday afternoon."

The woman snorted derisorily. "Ya know, it's funny. Last week was the anniversary of Adam...you know, I could have sworn I heard it. I was out in the field and there was a loud scream and then squealing tyres. I put it down to my imagination, I'd been thinking about Adam of course, but now..."

Saint turned his attention to Whitton and raised a brow. "Are you saying that you think you heard someone being run over last week? Outside the farm?"

Slowly, Audrey Whitman nodded.

Chapter Twelve

The walk back up the drive towards the road was treacherous, and Whitton cursed as she almost slid once more on the mud. "For fuck's sake. It's 80 degrees and everywhere else is baked half to death. How does this stay so bloody wet?"

"See, you're assuming it's mud." Saint grinned.

"Don't even joke. And make sure you take your shoes off before you get back in my car."

The road was quiet, a typical country lane that didn't get much traffic. Clumps of dried mud littered the tarmac where tractors and off-road vehicles had traversed. This side of the road had a long stretch of bushes six feet tall, maybe higher. They were taller than Whitton. Further along it became a wooden fence with chicken wire and then a wall. On the opposite side it was just trees all the way down in both directions. They arched over and across the road in parts, shaped by the height of HGVs that drove through. The nearest house wasn't in sight.

She kicked the mud from her shoes and looked left. "Okay I'll wander this way; you go that way. See if there is anything noteworthy." Taking the cigarettes from her pocket, she slid one from the packet and lit it as she walked, keeping to the right and facing any potential oncoming traffic. It was shadier on this side at least, and she covered almost half a mile before turning back.

When the farm came into sight, she could see Saint running back and waving at her. She kicked off and started running towards him.

"Fuck," he panted. "I couldn't get any signal." He waved his phone at her as he bent over to catch his breath. "I found her car. There's blood in it."

~Grave~

Both of them sat by the side of the road, watching as the white forensic vehicle finally pulled in. Uniform had closed off the road in both directions, a car stationed at each end. Saint groaned. "Bloody hell, it's Perkins."

"Just grin and bear it. We can leave now they're here."

They both stood and wandered over to the van as Dr. Clive Perkins jumped out from the passenger side, followed by Barry, his sidekick. "Good timing, DI Whitton." Perkins smirked. "I quite fancied a little jaunt today."

She stretched her neck from side to side and stood silently waiting as both men pulled on white Tyvek suits. She chuckled to herself as Perkins pulled the booties on over his dapper little shoes. Tiny feet. Now, she was looking at two slightly overweight, short, underwhelming men with clipboards. *Tweedle Dum and Tweedle Dee*, she thought.

"Think you found blood, eh?" Barry said with a wink and a little click of his tongue. "It's probably engine oil, or horse piss." He chuckled and she rolled her eyes.

"Yeah, you know us coppers, always dragging you guys out to investigate horse urine inside cars," she deadpanned and stared him down. She really didn't like these idiots much. She walked them over to the car, a 4 x 4 registered to Duncan Simmons, and they all stood looking at the blood-stained white leather seat. "I suppose it shouldn't take much to discover yay or nay, right?"

Perkins coughed to clear his throat before bending down and pulling a swab free of its packaging. He wiped it across the stained seat and stood up, holding it in the air as though this was his best magic trick. His magician's assistant, Barry the Pillock, pulled a small spray bottle of Luminol from his pocket and presented it like a rabbit coming out of a hat.

Whitton continued to glare. He smiled, the kind of smile that curdled milk, and then he pressed the spray and a fine mist covered the swab, turning it bright pink.

"Right, so we'll leave you to get on with sweeping this potential crime scene then, shall we?" Saint said, following Whitton, who had already turned and walked away.

"Like the tyre prints just here," she said, pointing out the obvious.

"No need to be quite so sarcastic, is there Whitton? We don't tell you how to do your job," Perkins retorted with a huff.

"True," she acknowledged. "But then, we know how to do our job." She didn't wait for a reply.

Chapter Thirteen

"So, what we know is this. Our suspect somehow comes into contact with the victim on Ashton Lane. Now, it's the same place where the Whitman farm is located. Not a coincidence, seeing as their son, Adam, was the boy Anita killed last year. Although a positive alcohol reading was taken at the time, it was never taken to court due to a technicality with the equipment, and Anita Simmons was never charged. If you study the crime scene photos, you'll also notice that it's Adam's grave that the killer has left the body on," Whitton explained to the team as the sound of gasps and muttered conversations ended the silence.

"Payback murder?" Bowen stated. "Someone's pissed off that she got away with it and decided to fix the problem."

Whitton shrugged. "Maybe, not ruling anything out right now."

A phone rang in the background, the noise barely audible now above the chatter of ideas and facts. Colleen shouted out, "Guv, phone for you."

Whitton nodded. "I'll be right back. Jeff, I want an update on CCTV from you, okay?"

"Sure." He smiled as she turned and walked into her office. Shutting the door behind her, she picked up the phone and pressed the button that would switch the call.

"DI Whitton."

"Hello Sophie." Whitton recognised the voice as that of DS Jackie O'Neil from Stratham. The small town was probably 30 miles away. "How are you?"

"Busy," she answered quickly. She didn't have time for a social call, especially not from Jackie.

"Still as intense, I always did find that quite sexy." She chuckled, eluding to their brief relationship years ago.

"Look, I don't want to be rude, but I am probably going to be. I don't have time for this. A woman was murdered last week."

Jackie sighed. "Yes, I heard about that. That's actually why I am calling."

"Go on."

"Oh, now you're interested." She started to laugh again and caught herself. "You'd probably be best off coming here, and I can give you all the details."

"Jackie, I really don't..."

"Constance Martin, ring any bells yet?"

Whitton sat up straight in her chair and picked up a pen. "She was my victim's client, killed herself."

"Yes, she did. I remember Anita from our investigation. That's what piqued my interest. However, the man whose body was left on Connie's grave last year, didn't kill *himself*."

"I'm on my way." She slammed the phone down and shouted for Dale. When he arrived at her door, she was already pulling on her jacket.

"That was Jackie O'Neil."

DS Saint groaned. "Jackie! Oh no."

"We need to go to Stratham; O'Neil's got another one. Find out everything you can about Constance Martin."

~Grave~

Stratham Nick was much like Woodington, only it was smaller. Stratham wasn't that big a town. The population of Woodington was just over one hundred thousand at the last census. In Stratham it was barely hitting fifty-five thousand. But it was considered the better area to live in, and so it had a police station and a small force to keep all of those big houses safe. O'Neil had transferred a few years back, and most people were grateful, especially Whitton.

Holding up her warrant card, Whitton asked the desk sergeant for DS O'Neil. She listened as the uniformed officer called up to the incident room and informed someone that DI Whitton was here to see DS O'Neil. She checked her watch and raised an eyebrow at Saint. They both knew O'Neil would keep them waiting.

Twelve minutes. It was quicker than Whitton thought it would be. Dale grinned at her as O'Neil strolled casually into the room. He too had been checking the time.

"Sophie." She smiled, a warm, hopeful smile. Then she saw Dale out of the corner of her eye and knew this was business only. "DS Saint." She inclined her head at him and then turned her attention back to Whitton. The smile was now gone, replaced with an air of professionalism and indifference.

They were led up a narrow flight of stairs, along a corridor, and then through two rooms until they finally came to a small office. Jackie O'Neil flung herself into a desk chair and rifled through some paperwork and files lying haphazardly on the top tray. Whitton took the chair opposite and placed her phone down on the desktop.

"So, tell me about Constance. We only know the name from a conversation with one of Anita's colleagues."

"We didn't get too far with it. Constance made an allegation about a George Herring. Nobody wanted to talk, not on the record anyway. It had been 25 years for most of his victims, but we hoped at least one would corroborate Connie's story ..." She lifted file after file until she found one and pulled it forward.

"Unfortunately, nobody would come forward and we had to let it drop. We all knew the old fucker was guilty. Should have seen Connie, a nervous wreck. Life had thrown nothing but shit at her, and it all started because of him."

"There's nothing on the system about a Constance Martin...Dale searched all records before we left." Whitton looked up from her notes, dark eyes intense as she stared across the desk.

"Well there wouldn't be, that wasn't her legal name. She said she had changed it by deed poll; I had no need to think she was lying. But anyway, she didn't, so she's recorded as Martin Tillerson by her arsehole family who didn't recognise her as female," O'Neil said, a little protectively.

"Okay, so Constance was transgender?"

Jackie nodded. "Yep, she was halfway through her transition when her counselling sessions brought up her past. After a lot of thought, she decided to report it. That's where she met Anita."

"What happened to Herring?"

"Found with a noose around his neck on Constance's grave. Six months ago."

"Any leads?"

O'Neil shook her head. "Nothing, we put it down to a friend maybe who decided to take the law into their own hands, but with no evidence it's just sat there in the cold case pile. Until I read through about your case – it's too damn similar to not be linked."

Chapter Fourteen

The office was quiet, as much as it could be with the continuous *tap tap* of keyboards and telephones ringing on unoccupied desks. It was stifling. There had been an argument earlier about whether it was cooler with the window open or closed. It had almost got to the point of fisticuffs when Whitton came into the office and shouted at them to pack it in. The fan wasn't touching it.

Now, they were coming up with every excuse to be out of the office. Patrol cars had never been more popular with the detectives.

Whitton yawned as she read for the fifth time that statistically, Woodington was the town with the smallest number of homeless. Whoever had come up with these numbers clearly didn't walk the streets at night counting the poor sods bunking down in any spot they could find that might be safe enough, warm enough, and dry. Constance Martin would certainly disagree if she were still alive.

The knock on the closed door jolted her from her thoughts. "Come in," she said, looking up at the door and closing the folder in front of her. She was still getting used to having her own office. She hadn't wanted it, but there had been a re-jig of space while she had been off work after the Doll Maker case, and now she was in here.

"Sorry, guv. There's a Gina Ashcroft downstairs, wants to talk to, and I quote, '*the fucker in charge of Darren Barton.*'" Colleen O'Leary smirked at her. "And..."

"Seeing as that fucker would be me..." Whitton smiled. "Okay, I'll be down in a minute. Stick her in an interview room."

She flicked through the pile of files stacked neatly on the corner of her desk. There were far too many of them. All were filled with gory details on some poor sod's early demise. Pulling out the file that was labelled Darren Barton, she skimmed through the information it held, which wasn't much. The medical report stated the facts. Witness reports where varied and contradictory. Darren started a fight; Darren didn't start the fight. It was three blokes, two blokes, a gang of people. All white, two black. It was all useless information, and none of it had provided a lead worth following up.

Jeff Branson had spent an entire afternoon going through CCTV. What was available was dark and grainy. Too many people were in the way to see a clear image of the actual stabbing, but they were following a few people around town via the CCTV system.

She slid the pages together and shuffled them into a tidy pile, stuffing them back into the cream-coloured folder. Pushing her chair back, she stood, shoved the file under her arm, and prepared herself for Gina Ashcroft.

~Grave~

Whitton opened the door to Interview Room 4 and found an irate Gina Ashcroft, red-faced and screaming at PC Carol Gardner. In an instant the woman turned her venom on Whitton.

"My Darren is dead and nobody is doing a fucking thing about it!"

Ignoring her, Whitton acknowledged Gardner with a nod. She closed the door and walked the three steps to the table. The onslaught of swear words and accusations continued as Whitton placed the file down on the table. "Take a seat, please," she demanded calmly before looking up to stare down the glare she was receiving.

Gina stood staring, all her weight on her left foot, hand on hip. "Who are you?" Her face contorted as she continued to chew on gum while speaking, chubby cheeks bulging with contempt.

Whitton repeated her request. "Sit down." She then pulled her own chair out and took a seat. Indignantly, the woman dragged the chair towards her, scraping the legs against the floor, before flopping into it with an audible huff. Whitton let her sit there in silence while she opened the folder and made a show of reading through it.

"Right, Ms. Ashcroft?" She looked up and waited for the woman to acknowledge her. She nodded, lips pursed together in an angry thin line. "My name is Detective Inspector Sophie Whitton. I am the lead investigator into Darren's death."

"Murder, he was murdered!" Gina screamed, launching herself forward in her seat. Spittle cascaded from her lips.

Whitton didn't flinch. This wasn't the first person to sit opposite her and try to intimidate her. Far from it, in fact; the tables were usually turned pretty quickly. "That may well turn out to be the case. Right now, I am only interested in the evidence, and we are currently in the early stages of gathering it."

"It's been nearly a week!" Gina shrieked again. Her face was flushed, angry and red. She looked bloated, like she had spent the week crying. Whitton's sympathy raised a notch.

Whitton sighed. "And we have been very active in seeking out witnesses. As you can see here." She held up the file and showed her. "Unfortunately, nobody has yet corroborated anybody else. So, we are looking into every possible lead we get, but unless we find something..."

"You'll just forget him. Chuck him on the cold case pile. He's just some Scrote from the estates, right? Nobody gives a fuck what happened to him." Gina thrust a chubby finger in Whitton's direction.

"Especially a stuck-up cow like you, think you're better than us just cos you've got a badge."

Whitton's dark eyes rested on her as she spoke. "I can assure you Ms. Ashcroft, that if the evidence is there, my colleagues will find it and I will bring those at fault to justice."

Gina sat back in her seat and folded her arms across her stomach defiantly. "Yeah, we will see."

Chapter Fifteen

Barnard's office door was open when Whitton arrived for an unscheduled meeting. Gina Ashcroft's impromptu visit had put Darren Barton in her mind, and it was interfering with her thought process over the Grave Deaths.

Knocking gently, she pushed the heavy door open and stepped inside. "Doc, do you have...?"

Standing in the middle of the room was a short bespectacled man, his chunky fingers wrapped around a file that was open as he perused the information.

"Can I help you, Detective Inspector?" Dr. Clive Perkins was a stuffy pain in the arse, as far as Whitton and her team were concerned. He was still considered new to Woodington, even though it had been almost two years, and so far, he hadn't endeared himself to many. He cut corners and guessed too often for her liking. She dealt in facts, and so did Barnard; that was why their conviction rates were some of the highest in the county. She rarely had to work with Perkins, thankfully. Barnard seemed to keep him on a short leash dealing with accidents and natural deaths mainly, for which Whitton was eternally grateful.

"Uh, I was hoping to speak with Doctor Barnard." She looked around the empty room. "Is he busy?"

He closed the file and placed it back down on the desk, where he obviously had found it. "I do believe that he is at a scene. Elderly gentleman, probably died of natural causes, but one can never be too sure nowadays, can we?" He was also a bit of a letch and wasn't shy about it. "Anything I can help you with?" He leered.

"Probably not," she muttered. "I just wanted to check there was nothing new on the Barton case?"

"Let me see, that's the chap who was stabbed at the pub last weekend?"

She nodded. "Yep. Seems cut and dried, but with no hard evidence there probably isn't too much we can do about getting a conviction. I was hoping something might have come up with the clothing?"

He smiled up at her. "Why don't we go and have a look then?" He walked past her towards the door. "Follow me." His eyes travelled the length of her, stopping briefly at the gap where her shirt was unbuttoned.

She rolled her eyes and cricked the muscle in her neck before grabbing the door as it shut and following the man as he all but ran down the hall to his own office, a room that couldn't be any more different from Barnard's. His furniture was modern, the kind you found in Ikea, not antiques like Barnard's. "Take a seat, I just need to…" He pressed a few keys on the computer. "Ah, there we go. Darren Barton?"

"Yes, stabbing."

He nodded, pulling out a different pair of spectacles that probably cost more than Whitton spent on a months' worth of food shopping. "There were a few strands of a red material. Synthetic. Dog hairs from...a Staffordshire Bull Terrier and an Alsatian. Not much else I am afraid." He continued to read down. "Have you any leads at all?" When he looked up, his line of sight fixed with her chest before finally meeting her eyes.

She shook her head. "No, I am hoping Jeff will find something on the CCTV. It happened in the centre of town. We must have images somewhere."

He took the glasses off and folded them carefully. "Well, I do hope you catch them. Nasty business."

She stood up. "Thanks, can you let Barnard know that I popped in?"

"Of course." He stood politely. "I hear you've linked the Grave murders?"

She considered telling him to mind his own fucking business. "Yes. It appears we have a vigilante on our hands."

He nodded and smiled, chubby cheeks reddening. "Well, if I can ever help, do let me know." Highly doubtful on both counts, she thought.

"Results back on the blood from Ashton Lane yet?"

He looked back at the computer, putting his glasses back on. Hit a few more keys and read the report. "Yes, we can confirm that it was in fact Anita Simmons' blood."

~Grave~

She stalked into the squad room and threw her coat down on her old desk before flopping down into the empty chair. "Ugh, I feel violated."

"Lucky you," grinned Dale. "I haven't been violated for days; this heat is playing havoc with my nocturnal interests."

She grimaced. "I'm just going to think of Becky naked when you say things like that, you know that, right?"

He laughed out loud and pulled his feet down from the desk.

"Perkins," was all she said.

"Oh, grim. Even I feel violated when I have to deal with him."

She switched on the computer and pulled some files from her bag. "Count yourself lucky that you don't have breasts for him to stare at."

The computer screen lit up her face as it booted up. "You do know you have an actual office now, don't you?" Bowen said as he passed the desk and stopped to nab a biscuit from the box on Dale's desk.

She looked up at him and batted her eyes dramatically. "But I miss you so much."

"It's the aftershave, right?" he joked.

Dale grinned and stood up. He walked across the room and opened the window as far as it would go. His shirt stuck to his back. It was humid and sticky, the kind of day that only a bath of ice was going to soothe.

"Anyway." She yawned as she spoke. "Blood's a match, it was Anita's. He took her from the scene of her own crime."

"So, he is either in the car with her already or..." Dale thought out loud.

"Maybe he did a Ted Bundy." Bowen said, shoving another custard cream into his mouth. When all he got were vacant stares, he added, "You know, pretended he was hurt, or had a puncture. She slows down to help and bam." He slapped the desk with his palm. "Shoves her face into the steering wheel, she's dazed, he takes the opportunity and puts her in his own car."

Whitton nodded. "Completely plausible. And would mean it was someone she knew."

Whitton stared up at the photo of Anita Simmons on the murder board. She had been an attractive woman with warm brown eyes and a big smile. She looked like the kind of woman you could sit down with and have a chin wag over coffee. "I want to find the person that did this to her," she said, her lips pursed and nostrils flared. "Two kids are motherless…"

Bowen and Saint were silent; they all had the same thoughts on the case.

Chapter Sixteen

Whitton looked up before Jeff knocked on the open door. "Guv, I've got something on the CCTV re the Barton case."

"Okay." She indicated the seat in front of her desk and he stepped forwards, dropping into the chair. Sweat rolled slowly down his forehead and a sweat stain marked his shirt. "What have you got?" she asked, sitting back in her chair and giving him her attention.

"Trevor Hayes and Tyler Jacobs. I've got a clear image of both of them arguing with Darren earlier that day outside of M&S." Both men were known to the police, the kind of men that found themselves regularly inside a cell or being at the forefront of a copper's thoughts when looking into any petty theft or, in this case, a fight.

"Right."

"So, it got physical, but a couple of PCSOs walking through put a stop to it before it got out of hand." She waited, expressionless, until he continued. "Right, so instead of following Darren, I followed them. They hung around in town most of the day at various places. Coffee shops, the betting shop on Dean Street." He shrugged. "Anyway, they ended up at the King's Head about thirty minutes before Darren arrived."

Now, she was more interested. She sat up and wiped her face with her hand. "Go on."

"It's not clear cut, but just before the fight kicked off, they moved in."

"They got any form for using weapons?"

He nodded. "I'll get the files."

"Okay, leave them with me, then take Andy with you and pick one of them up." She turned her attention back to Dale. "Thank God for Police Community Support Officers, eh?"

~Grave~

Constance Martin lived an upbeat life really, considering all that she had been through. Whitton was early and read through her file as she waited in the car to speak with her parents. Born Martin Julian Tillerson, she had done well at school. Studied hard and got a job in a local bank. At first, it appeared that Martin had attempted to live a life that fit. She dated several men, but none of the relationships seemed to work out. At 28, Martin began the process of transitioning physically into Constance. The progression was slow and tiresome if you needed the NHS. Constance had taken to prostitution in order to speed up the procedures by going private. What little Whitton knew about being transgender or the treatments involved had come from TV and newspapers, or the diversity courses she got sent on.

She made a mental note to speak to someone for more information. Checking her watch, she closed the file, placed it back in her bag, and got out of the car.

Martin Tillerson Sr wasn't the kind of man who Whitton assumed would be all that pleased to discover his child was anything but straight and cisgender. Mrs. Tillerson, or Barbara, looked as though she was a woman who believed in her husband, especially his right to rule the roost. Other than a quick hello, she didn't speak. It was awkward, and probably the only time that Whitton wished she had Dale with her.

"So, I wanted to speak to you face-to-face. We have an ongoing case open right now involving Constance," Whitton said as she took a seat at the dining room table made of dark mahogany polished to within an inch of its life.

"Who?" the father asked. His face was passive as he stared at her, big hands folded around one another on the table.

"Constance Martin, she was formerly…"

"You mean Martin, our son?" She remembered the photo of Constance and considered how unfortunate she was that she looked like her father. Except the eyes; Constance didn't have his mean, glowering brow and cold, staring eyes. She had her mother's. Warm, but wary.

Whitton didn't answer. Instead she looked at the wife, who looked away.

"I wondered what you could tell me about George Herring?"

The wife looked to the husband for answers. "Not sure I can tell you anything," he said. "We never met him more than a handful of times. He seemed nice enough."

"Were you aware that Constance had made a complaint to the police about him?

"Why would we be aware of that?" Not, why would she do that? Whitton wasn't sure this man knew the first thing about his child.

Barbara Tillerson finally spoke. "W-what kind of complaint?"

"Sexual assault, as a child." She wasn't going to pull her punches with these people. Barbara Tillerson's face went white.

"I suppose that explains why he was the way that he was," Mr. Tillerson said, straightening up and puffing his chest out, as though somehow having a reason like that was better than accepting your kid might just be trans, like it was less of a reflection on him.

Holding her tongue once more, Whitton pressed on. "So, I am trying to gain more information on—"

"The thing is, Officer—"

"Detective, it's Detective Inspector Whitton," she interrupted. She was a little tired of people like this: self-righteous and pious.

"Right, well the thing is you see, we didn't really see very much of Martin once he left home. And if we're honest, we preferred it that way than to witness him behaving the way that he was. Wearing skirts and dresses, it's not natural." He tried to smile, and Whitton ignored him. Smiling at him would give him the impression that she agreed, and she didn't. She might not understand much about Constance's decisions in life, but she understood her right to make them and to live them.

She stood up and grabbed her bag. "I just wanted you to know that I will do whatever I can for *Constance*." She asserted the name and made it clear that was whose side she was on. "Her attacker may well be dead now, but if I can prove what he did..." She left it there. "Whatever you think? Constance was still your child."

~Grave~

The office was loud when Whitton came back. Andy Bowen and Jeff Branson were celebrating.

Someone had opened another large box of biscuits on the desk and filled the coffee machine with a fresh brew. She filled a mug and contemplated the scene.

Andy grinned and raised his coffee cup. "We got them," he announced. "Trevor Hayes and Tyler Jacobs," he reminded her – not that she had forgotten, but she let him carry on. "Hayes flipped."

Jeff butted in then, his own grin wide and bright. "Yeah, he decided that Jacobs was a good mate, but he wasn't worth going to prison for."

"So, you've got it all wrapped up then?" she asked, taking a sip of her coffee.

Both men nodded. "Signed and sealed. The CPS seem happy with it. Both were charged with manslaughter this morning."

She turned and headed towards her office. "If anyone wants me, I'll be visiting Gina Ashcroft with the news, and then I am going home.

Chapter Seventeen

Whitton stretched out on the couch, surrounded by paper held down with every object she could find to stop it blowing away when the oscillating fan swept back around the room. It was gone nine p.m., and the Chinese take-away she had ordered on the way home was still in its containers on the counter in a white plastic bag, forgotten.

She was expecting Rachel at some point. The nurse had been due to finish her shift around seven, but an RTA involving three cars had meant she was requested to stay on, much to Whitton's distress. She wanted her here. To keep herself busy, she had started reading through all of the files she had on both Grave cases.

The file on Constance Martin was open and spread out in front of her. Jackie had been right when she had said there wasn't much. Witness statements barely filled half a page. She stretched out and let her head fall back against the couch. Her eyes were gritty, tired from the lack of sleep these past few nights. She fished out the autopsy report from amongst the photographs of the body in situ and then the autopsy shots, and started to read through.

She skipped through the usual data regarding height, weight, etc., and found the cause of death: suicide by hanging. The pathologist also noted a large fist-sized bruise to the abdominal area, as well as bruising to the left side of the victim's zygomatic arch and supraorbital ridge. Constance had been beaten.

The key sliding into the lock got her attention, and she placed the paperwork back into the file, grabbing at the rest and tidying it all away just as the door swung open and Rachel slumped in. "Hey," she called out as she hung her jacket on the hook Saint had put up for Sophie. She dropped her bag down on the floor.

"Alright, how was work?" Sophie said, standing and moving towards the kitchen to head Rachel off. The blonde pressed a kiss to the corner of her mouth as soon as she reached her.

"Was okay, just busy, you know. I thought I was going to get away on time, and then..." She didn't need to go into details; Sophie knew all she needed to know.

"Wanna brew?" The kettle was already filled and ready to go when Sophie flicked the switch for it to boil. She turned, her back leant up against the counter. Rachel smiled and casually stepped into her space, her arms easily snaking around her lover's neck as she brought their lips together. The gentleness with which the kiss began was almost torturous as Sophie let her hands rest gently around Rachel's waist, deepening the kiss with an unhurried and leisurely nipping of her lips until they parted to allow the slow intrusion of her tongue to slide effortlessly against its match. At the touch, Rachel groaned and parted her legs, one either side of Sophie's thigh. Heat and steam from the kettle brought a sheen of sweat to her skin.

"Mm, kiss me like that always," Rachel whispered as they parted, her forehead resting against Sophie's lips.

"Supraorbital bridge, that's the eyebrow, right?" Sophie said.

Rachel leant back and raised a perfectly shaped supraorbital bridge. "Okay, random. But, yes." She couldn't keep the grin from her face as she traced her finger along Sophie's brow. Sophie in work mode was pretty much her favourite, other than Sophie in sex mode; that Sophie always won out. "Why?" She stepped back so that Sophie could turn and finish making a cup of tea, the kettle having clicked to announce its achievement moments earlier.

"Just reading through an autopsy, and the vic had bruising to that and the zygomatic arch, which I do know is the cheekbone," she answered before Rachel could tell her that. Teabags drenched in boiling water, she turned back around to allow them to steep a little. "I'm guessing she was involved in a fight at some point just before she died. Probably has nothing to do with the case, just feel for her."

Rachel moved back in and took up the same position as before, straddling her detective's leg. "Is this related to the Grave Murders?"

Sophie pulled on Rachel's hips, needing to feel closer. "Maybe. Are you hungry? I picked up Chinese."

"Death to food in less than a minute." Rachel chuckled. "Don't let that tea stew." She winked and pulled away. "I'm just going to grab a shower and change."

~Grave~

Rachel wanted her, that much was clear as she rhythmically undulated her hips back and forth, impaled upon the rigid digits Sophie held firm between her thighs. Rachel's palms pressed down against Sophie's chest, kneading and squeezing her lover's breasts. She plied taut nipples between her fingers and felt her own wetness increase. *This* was her new favourite position, of which there had been many.

"Don't move," Rachel pleaded, her eyes rolling and flickering closed as she felt Sophie hit that sweet spot. She clenched her knees tighter to Sophie's slim frame, holding her hostage as she used every inch of those dexterous fingers to her advantage.

Sophie's face was in awe of her as she watched Rachel take what she needed. A sheen of sweat glistened across her skin and sparkled under the dimming light. Tiny droplets making their way down her brow to drip onto Sophie's hot skin. She was sure she heard it sizzle. Full breasts bounced gently. It was the image that Sophie enjoyed most.

Rachel was going to come; she was clear about that. She knew that Sophie had felt it, the natural tightening around her fingers and the added lubrication, but watching Sophie as her muscles tightened, her back arching as she cried out, was almost enough to push her over the edge again.

Rachel's eyes locked onto her as she lowered down to share a kiss. Her palms moved up, resting either side of Sophie's head as she began to move again, thrusting more powerfully than before as the echoes of a second orgasm reverberated off the walls. "Don't hold back," Sophie whispered breathlessly against Rachel's lips.

"I won't," she all but hissed. She kept her eyes locked firmly on Sophie. Her palms reached for her cheeks, and she held Sophie's face in place. "I love how you feel inside me." Her movements stuttered. Sophie shifted her thumb and pressed harder against Rachel's most sensitive spot. "Fuck." Her breath caught in her throat. Sophie's right arm reached around her waist, pulling her closer, fingers splayed, holding her as she increased the pressure and edged her into one orgasm after another. Rachel felt Sophie's grip on her tighten as her body contorted, twisting and bending at will as pure pleasure coursed through her cells, searching out every nerve ending before finally she sagged against Sophie, bringing their mouths together again. Sloppy, intense kisses deepened and kept their arousal spiking. Sophie wanted nothing more than to gorge herself on this sweating, heaving mess of beautiful flesh.

Rachel pulled away, smiling at her. Her left hand rested still on Sophie's bony shoulder. Her other hand dipped between them, between her legs. She found herself and began to slowly tease. Sophie's eyes dropped lower, enticed and entranced by her insatiable lover. "You do this to me," Rachel said, her voice husky and sexier than Sophie had ever heard it. "Just you." She brought her fingers to her lips and sucked them clean. "Taste me," she whispered, leaning forward to kiss her lover.

Sophie moaned out loud, her lover's essence invading her senses. "Come up here." she demanded, breaking the kiss and sliding lower into the bed. Rachel rose up to meet her, her pelvis thrusting forward at the first touch of Sophie's soft lips as she kissed her right there, between her thighs, exploring Rachel with every featherlight sweep of her tongue. Sophie's palms gripped rounded buttocks, pulling her closer, always closer.

~Grave~

Rachel rested her head against her lover's chest as they lay together in the dark. "What are you thinking about?" she asked dreamily. Fully sated and relaxed, she could envisage a life like this.

"You, us," Sophie replied.

"Hmm, what about us?"

Sophie let her fingers pull gently through Rachel's hair. "I dunno, just...I'm seeing a doctor."

"What kind of doctor?"

"The head doctor kind." She felt better saying it out loud.

Rachel tried not to react. She'd been waiting for this moment, when Whitton would finally let Sophie deal with the shit storm that they had been through.

"You don't seem surprised?"

Thinking carefully, Rachel replied, "I'm just glad that you felt you could tell me."

"I wasn't going to...I just decided then that I should. Dr. Westbrook says that we should talk...You know, about..."

"Anthony?"

Sophie nodded. "Yeah," she whispered. Rachel moved, leaning up on her elbow to face Sophie, who searched Rachel's face. "I see you...when I'm at crime scenes...when there is..." She swallowed and closed her eyes. When they opened again and found the green looking back at her, she continued. "I keep seeing you, lifeless. When there is a body, it's you that my brain processes."

"What does Dr. Westbrook say?" Rachel's fingertips stroked lovingly around Sophie's stomach.

"She says I need to forgive myself, that it wasn't my fault and I need to accept that."

"And you don't?"

Whitton shook her head. "No, I should have…" She blinked back tears. "I should have worked it out faster, I should have…I should have read the clues better and…"

"Do you know what I was thinking in those moments?"

Sophie shook her head, unsure if she even wanted to hear it, but she deserved to. She deserved to hear how she had let her lover down.

Rachel took her hand and interlocked their fingers. "I was thinking, if anyone is going to save me, it's going to be Sophie. I never had any doubts that you would come. Even when I felt his hands around…"

"Shit!" Sophie cried out as the tears finally flowed. She knew what Anthony had done, of course she did, she had read all the reports, but hearing it from her lover's own lips was just too much.

Rachel gripped her hand tighter. "I don't blame you; I blame him. I blame my parents, the boy at his school who hurt him. I blame a multitude of people, but never, not once have I ever blamed you, Sweetheart." Pulling their joined hands towards her, she kissed them. "You're my hero. My person, the only one that I can truly just let go with. Anthony was sick, depraved and mentally unstable. He is the one that hurt me, not you. Never you."

Chapter Eighteen

Chief Inspector Adam Turner's office was cool. A small air con unit had been wheeled in earlier in preparation for the meeting. Whitton sat opposite with a mug of coffee in her hand, wondering why Dale had been looking at her oddly earlier. Two flat tan-coloured files lay in her lap, and she fingered the corner of one where it curled slightly.

Looking around the office, she realised how sterile her own was. His was filled with photographs of a wife and three children. Even the family dog had made it into a frame and was given pride of place alongside the others on a shelf just behind him. There was another shelf full of law books. She wondered if he ever read them or if they were just there for show. Stifling a yawn as his monotone voice waffled on to whoever it was that he was speaking to, she tried not to listen in. It wasn't work related, that much was clear. She lifted the mug and took a swig as she waited for her superior to finish his phone call.

She was still getting used to having her own office. She hadn't asked for it and she was still unsure if she even liked it. She spent most of her time in the main office like always. Maybe that was why she had done nothing to make it more her own. It had a desk, some filing cabinets, and three chairs. The shelves were empty but for the piles of cold cases files that she kept to hand. Any quiet moment she would spend going over one of them, hoping maybe she would spot something that was missed before, but it rarely happened.

Turner put the phone down at the same time Sophie rested her mug back on the desk. She fidgeted and got herself settled in her seat once more before clearing her throat.

"Sir."

"Sorry about that," he said, indicating the call. "Thanks for being so prompt." He sat back in his chair and looked at her. "So, where are we on the Barton case?"

"As of now, it's all wrapped up on our end. Bowen and Branson did a sound job of tracking down the CCTV to create a well-put-together case against Trevor Hayes and Tyler Jacobs. Both have form for violence."

"Right, and the Doc confirms everything?"

Whitton nodded. "Yep, DNA confirms that both were there at the time. Barton's blood was found on a pair of trainers and a jacket worn by Jacobs. Hayes admitted to being there and helping Jacobs to get rid of the knife."

Turner breathed deeply and nodded. "Excellent, let CPS deal with it then. What about this grave business?"

Whitton changed files. Opening it, she pulled out the first page and passed it across to Turner. "Right now, we have another case that seems to link into this. As you can see, the victim in each case lies on top of the grave of their alleged victim."

"Alleged?"

Whitton licked her bottom lip as she pulled two other pieces of paper from the file and passed them across. "George Herring was found last year on top of the grave of one of his alleged victims. No charges were brought against him in a historic child abuse case against Constance Martin, also known as Martin Tillerson. Constance was transgender, however with the court case and other things going on in her life, she hadn't gone any further into legally changing her name or getting a gender recognition certificate sorted, and that meant her delightful parents were able to totally disregard her as a woman."

He perused the information, quickly scanning the page before looking up. "So they buried her as a him, Martin Tillerson?"

Tilting her head, Whitton scrunched up her face in annoyance. "Yes. I met with them. They are insistent that Constance was their *son*...I may have overstepped the mark."

Turner sat up straight; he was used to his DI and the way that she worked. He listened. "Go on."

"I told them that regardless of whether she was Constance or Martin, she was still their child." Shrugging, she added, "I think they were aware that I wasn't impressed with them."

"Well, if they make a complaint then I will deal with it, otherwise, I wouldn't worry too much. I won't be kowtowing to a couple of bigots. Tell me about Anita Simmons."

She nodded; it helped having a superior on your side. "Anita was left on the grave of Adam Whitman. She was involved in an RTA last year, and Adam was the victim. It was an accident from what I can tell, but the breathalyser unit used at the scene recorded Anita as being over the limit. She accepted that she had had a drink, but only the one. It was then discovered that the unit hadn't been calibrated correctly, and the evidence was thrown out. Anita Simmons was free to go. Both cases are also connected in that Anita Simmons was also Constance Martin's sexual assault adviser."

"So what's the thinking on the whole?" he asked, sitting back in his chair again.

"I think we have a vigilante on the loose. Someone who has deemed themselves judge, jury, and executioner."

"So it seems." He steepled his hands together.

"Whoever it is, is smart. There is barely any forensic evidence. These deaths are happening with no witnesses. We don't have much to go on other than hoping he, or she, makes a mistake the next time."

"I want to be kept up to date with this, Whitton. If we have something more sinister on our hands, then I want us concentrating all our efforts on containing it as quickly as possible."

"Sure. Might help if the rest of the department could have one of these." She smiled pointedly towards the air con unit.

Chapter Nineteen

Outside Woodington Magistrates Court, Whitton lit up a cigarette and blew out a white puff of air. She wanted to be here early and get in to see the CPS solicitor beforehand. She had a file of evidence to pass over and would be watching the proceedings from the back, unable to give any evidence until the pair were passed on to the Crown Court.

She watched as Gina Ashcroft arrived, supported on either side by two equally somber women. A black veil covered her face in an overly dramatic attempt at showing the world her grief. All three glared at Whitton as they passed by on the steps. She couldn't make out their whispered comments, but the detective knew they were aimed at her. She was used to it; it didn't matter to her what they thought. Her colleagues had done their jobs, found the evidence, and passed it on. Whatever Gina and her cronies thought, it wasn't the police they should be angry with. Hayes and Jacobs would both be remanded.

Stubbing her cigarette out on the metal box attached the wall, she dropped the butt inside. As she was about to step inside, a man followed her in, almost knocking her over.

"Oh, I am so sorry..." His dark eyes found hers, and recognition appeared between them both. "DS Whitton, how are you?"

Jonas Robinson was greying around the hairline a little, not quite as slim as he had been a few years ago when she remembered seeing him last. Hitting his fifties had clearly taken its toll, or was it the stress of the job?

"Jonas, good to see you. I'm well, thanks, and it's DI now." She smiled a thin smile. "How are you?"

He smoothed down his suit jacket and stood straight-backed, his full height not quite as tall as Whitton, but his northern accent was still as strong as ever. "I should have known you'd have moved up the ranks. I'm well, thanks. Just here to drop off some papers and then hang around. I'm duty solicitor today. You know how it is, always someone to defend." He emptied his pockets and handed his briefcase over before walking through the metal detector. "Same faces every day sometimes."

"Yes, unfortunately they don't seem to always learn their lessons, do they?" She smiled at him again and then checked her watch. She still had a few minutes, but followed him in anyway, emptying her own pockets into the tray. "So, I haven't seen you for what? 10 years? What are you doing here? London not exciting enough anymore?"

"Has it been that long?" He grinned in return. "We moved back a while ago. My wife has family here, so it made things easier, but I was commuting until recently." He shrugged. "Have enjoyed my travels, but eventually you have to put down roots, don't you?"

"Married now then too?" Whitton asked, not really that interested, but she had liked him, back in the day. She had learned a lot from people like him. He had always been a stickler for the rules and carried the fierce belief that everybody deserved a defender.

His face lit up then. "Yes, Lydia, she's a vet, runs her own practice from home. We met at a St John's Ambulance course about five years ago, married for four."

"That's great. I know who to call should I ever get a pet."

He smiled. "Anyway, I should get on. You here on a case?"

"Yep, two-hander: Jacobs and Hayes, routine stabbing. They're finger-pointing, so I'm dragged down here, along with Branson, to talk about CCTV evidence." She shrugged.

"Guilty?"

She glared a little at him. "Of course, we don't bring charges against innocent people, regardless of what you defense lawyers think."

He grinned. "Touché. Let's hope the right result rings true then." She nodded, her attention then caught by the good-looking black guy waving at her from outside. "I'll see you around then," he said quickly as he dashed towards Court Three.

Whitton nodded, turned her attention to the notice board and running a finger down the lists of cases to be heard, just as Jeff came to stand beside her. Hayes. Trevor. Court Two, second on the list. "Court Two."

"Yep. Who was that?"

"Someone I knew from my time in London. Jonas Robinson, nice guy, bit of a do-gooder. You know the type, always looking out for the ones we put away," she added before turning and bounding up the stairs. "You're cutting it fine, by the way." She glanced at her watch once more. They had a couple of minutes to get inside and in place before the magistrates appeared.

"Yeah, sorry. I set the alarm clock, but there was a power cut in the night."

Rolling her eyes, she said, "Get a wind-up one then."

The courtroom itself was bright and airy. It had high ceilings with windows either side that ran the length of the wall. They were ushered in by Tom, he'd been doing that job since God was a boy. "Take a seat, officers," he said, pointing over to the area they already knew they would be sitting in. In front of the gallery, but behind the prosecution desk.

"I just need a word with Ms. Akim," Whitton said, nodding toward the prosecuting team. She wandered over and tapped the short woman on the shoulder. "Sorry, Ms. Akim? DI Whitton. Lead on the Jacob and Hayes Case."

"Oh right, good morning, Detective." There was a small smile that crept across her lips, but it didn't stay put; instead a frown appeared. "Did you not get the message?

"No, what message?"

She looked a little flustered. "I...we...we don't need you to give evidence today. I think Jacobs going to Crown will be a given without the need for..." She smiled again and took her seat, turning back to face her laptop.

"Sorry, what do you mean?"

Ms. Akim had no time to answer as the court legal adviser stood. "Would the court stand?" Whitton glared down at the prosecutor but backed away as soon as the judge entered.

"Good morning, be seated," the judge said cheerfully, smiling in Whitton's direction. "What do we have on the list this morning?" Judge Renton was considered a fair and honest woman in most circles. Whitton was always grateful to see her sitting on the bench for any of her cases. Though in her sixties, she looked much younger. Her short blonde hair was beautifully styled, and she wore just enough make-up.

The people around her began to list the names of the cases due to be brought in front of her that morning. Whitton stewed. Sensing the irritation, Branson ventured a whispered question. "What's wrong?"

The DI leant in and whispered back, "I think they're letting Hayes go."

"What?" Branson half-whispered a little too loudly. The prosecution legal aid and the court usher both turned and glared at him. "How can they?"

Her jaw tensed, lips thinly pressed together. "I guess we are about to find out," she hissed.

The first case on the list was quickly adjourned when it became apparent that the man in question had had some kind of episode in the cells and was deemed unfit to attend. Hayes and Jacobs were up next. Standing in the dock before toughened glass, Hayes sported a black eye and Jacobs looked angry. They stood as far apart from one another as they could. Hayes was in a cheap suit, two sizes too big and obviously borrowed from a friend. Jacobs wore jeans and a t-shirt.

They both confirmed names, addresses, dates of birth and their nationality when requested by the legal advisor. "Who is representing Mr. Jacobs?"

"I am, sir." A man in smart suit stood and addressed the court. "Gordon Black," he said for the record, though everyone knew who Gordon Black was: the biggest scumbag defense lawyer in Woodington. He wore Saville Row, with initialed cufflinks, and thought nothing of representing any and every criminal without a solicitor. He wasn't interested in them, just the payday they brought for a few minutes' work.

"And who is representing Mr. Hayes?" The man looked around the room until a tall woman wearing a baggy cardigan stood. "I am, sir. Margaret Connelly."

With all the details noted, he read out the charge and both men answered that they understood. It was at that point that Ms. Connelly stood and made her case.

"Your Honour, I have spoken previously with my learned friend and discussed the case in depth. I think if you look at the evidence, although nobody disagrees that my client was in fact there when the incident took place, it is also evident that he was not the perpetrator of the crime. And as he has also been very forthcoming in giving evidence, of which I believe the prosecution has built most of its case on…I would, if it pleases the court, ask that the charge of manslaughter be dropped against my client."

"No, they killed him! Both of them!" screamed Gina from behind Whitton.

"Sit down please, may I remind you that this is a court of law? Any further outbursts will see you removed from court," the judge said from her seat high above them all. She turned her attention to Akim. "Does the prosecution have any counter argument to put forward?"

Standing, Ms. Akim shook her head. "No, your honour. We believe that although we have a case against Mr. Hayes, it would be prudent to use his testimony as a witness against Mr. Jacobs, who we believe was the actual perpetrator in the murder of Darren Barton. We may look to bring a lesser charge of affray at a later date."

"I see, then if you are both satisfied, Mr. Hayes, is granted an NFA for now." The judge then turned to the dock and to Hayes. "Mr. Hayes, with no further action to answer for today, you are free to go."

Whitton stared up at the coat of arms on the wood paneling. The unicorn and the lion stood proudly on either side of the royal standard. Every court had one; she looked on it as a symbol of justice. Now as the smiling figure of Trevor Hayes was released from the dock. She wondered just whose justice it was.

~Grave~

"I don't fucking believe it," Jeff Branson ranted and tossed the phone onto the desk as soon as they'd returned to the office. "They're dropping the case against Hayes."

"What?" Bowen said, standing up with his face contorted. "How the hell? He was there."

Whitton watched the scene play out in front of her. Branson was still just as pissed now as when the judge had read out the ruling, and she couldn't blame him. He had spent hours going through the CCTV and putting together the evidence they needed, some of it in his own time.

"Yeah, he was there, but not enough evidence to say he *actually* caused Barton's death, plus he is now a prosecution witness against Jacobs. They'd rather guarantee one conviction, than risk losing both."

Whitton moved past them, dropped her bag down on her old desk, and flopped into the vacant chair.

"And that bloody witch attacked the Guv," Jeff stated. All eyes turned towards Whitton. She had her feet up on the desk, her eyes closed. The silence of the room now indicated that she was expected to reply.

"Attacked is a little bit of an over statement." She opened her eyes and, one leg at a time, placed her feet back on the ground. "The woman was upset, she's lost her partner and one of his killers is getting away with it, scot free. I think she's entitled to be a little pissed."

"Come on, Guv. She launched herself at you, another inch closer and you'd be wearing a shiner." Jeff grinned, remembering back to the way Whitton had sidestepped Gina's fist and still managed to stop the woman from falling and landing on her arse. The court officials had quickly escorted her from the building before she got a charge of contempt of court and a few hours cooling off in the cells.

"Thankfully, I'm not."

"Shame." Dale smirked. "A nurse at home, too."

He ducked just in time to avoid the Bic pen that flew past his head. "I don't need an injury for my partner to pay me attention." She grinned.

Chapter Twenty

Whitton's desk phone rang. Dale answered it as she glanced up at the time; almost four p.m. She listened as he spoke.

"Yeah, okay, send him up."

She turned away from the computer mumbling, "Fuck sake, who wants to bug me now?!"

"Some cop from Croydon. Says he has something of interest." He shrugged and stood up, stretching out his back and arms.

"Better put the kettle on then," she said, yawning.

It didn't take long before DI Richard Chivers strolled into the incident room with all the confidence of a man that took no shit. Tall and built like a rugby player, his dark eyes scanned the room before settling on her. "You must be Whitton."

Whitton raised a brow. "I must be, and you are?"

"Chivers, DI Richard Chivers." She almost laughed at the James Bond-style introduction. "I wanted to come here personally rather than do it over the phone." He perched himself on the corner of a desk and held the files he carried across his middle.

"Coffee?" Dale called out and received a nod in return.

Whitton leant her weight to one foot. Crossing her arms over her chest, she waited.

His smile was charming, but wasted on her, and he knew it. "So, we have a case that fits your grave murders."

Saint brought three cups of coffee over and handed them out. "Go on," Whitton urged.

"Cathy Owumbi was a 69-year-old Nigerian woman who had settled in the UK 25 years ago. She took citizenship in 2001 and trained to become a psychiatric nurse, working in Croydon. She was killed in a hit and run on her way home from a late shift in 2015. The car was found two days later, and it took another week for forensics to run down the evidence and bring Paul Crawford to our attention. The car was stolen, and although Crawford's DNA put him inside the car, the evidence was tainted when someone at the lab mixed up the labels. Even though the labs re-ran the tests, it was enough to put doubt on the table, and he was acquitted." He shrugged and shook his head. "She was a good woman. Her gravestone in Croydon is where the body of Paul Crawford was found on January 18th 2016." He handed her the two files.

Inside was a photograph of an elderly black woman, full of life, smiling at the camera. She had a gap between her front two teeth and wore her hair neatly beneath a brightly coloured scarf. Behind it was another photograph of the same woman, but this time there was no smile. Instead, she was laid out across the road, her head resting on the kerb; a concrete pillow. Whitton read the medical report, the list of injuries, and silently closed the file.

"I'll add Cathy to the board," she said solemnly, receiving a nod and half a smile from Chivers. She opened the second file and came face to face with Paul Crawford's mugshot. He looked bleary-eyed, gaunt and unconcerned. There were photos of the car and then crime scene photos of Crawford's body in situ at the graves and during autopsy. Evidence was recorded on sheets of paper, along with medical recordings from the ME, all of which she scanned quickly before passing both files to Dale. Saint opened each one and perused it while Whitton continued on. "So, we have three now."

"That we know of," Chivers added. "Whoever did this is smart, they know what they are doing. They've got balls to carry it out and they leave us nothing forensically."

"So you think they've done this before?" she asked, sipping her coffee.

He picked his own mug up and took a sip. "I think it's a possibility, and they probably won't stop."

"Yes, a vigilante killer, someone who believes they are doing what is right. They're not killing for fun, it's not a compulsive need for them. Killing isn't the aim. Righting wrong, that's what they want to achieve."

"I hope you don't mind, but when I heard about your cases, I sent out a few feelers to some colleagues. Maybe we will get lucky and find out someone else knows something about this."

Dale finished pinning the photos up. Turning back to Whitton and Chivers, he added, "If we're lucky, he wasn't always quite so gifted in covering his footprints."

"Right, well you're welcome to hang around, but I'm sure you've got plenty to keep you busy back in Croydon," Whitton said, dismissing Chivers politely.

Chapter Twenty-One

With Rachel showering, Sophie took the opportunity to check her phone. She pulled a vest on and picked the gadget up from where she had left it on the kitchen table. Rachel's cottage was different now. Long gone were all the trinkets and ornaments of her past, things her brother had sullied when he had tried to kill her. She had needed some order, and where her home had once been a cluttered, lived-in abode, it was now a sterile and blank canvas ready to begin collecting new trinkets and memories. Rachel had tried to explain that she was exorcising demons. Sophie wasn't sure why she stayed here at all anymore; maybe it *was* time they moved in together.

There were no messages or missed calls, and she dropped the phone back down on the worktop, grateful that for once that she might get to spend an entire evening with her girlfriend that wasn't interrupted by murder and mayhem.

"Rachel, come on, we're going to be late," Sophie called out as she pulled on a pair of lightweight cargo pants. She could hear the hairdryer switch on and rolled her eyes. She checked her wallet and noted the lack of notes. A quick trip to the ATM would be delaying them even more. If it was just the two of them, then she would pay for it with her debit card, but they were meeting Becky and Dale, and her partner would insist on splitting the bill.

They had been doing this almost weekly for the last six months. Ever since The Doll Maker case. Whitton and Saint had always worked well together, but something clicked between them on that case, and now Dale Saint was about as good a friend as Sophie had ever had. Becky and Rachel also worked together, and so the foursome had become something of an easy routine they all enjoyed.

The restaurant was booked for eight o'clock. Usual time, usual place. It was now quarter to, and being late flustered Whitton. Rachel never seemed bothered if they were late, especially when Sophie had walked through the door and taken her straight to bed.

In her last relationship, Sophie never felt like Yvonne was that bothered if they had sex at all. If they had plans, then the last thing Yvonne would consider was going to bed and working off some of the day's stress. That made it easy for Sophie to just ignore it too. She became rigid and disinterested. With Rachel, things were different, and Sophie liked it like that. The power dynamics between them shifted naturally and easily, with the blonde easily circumventing any protest Sophie might put up.

When Rachel finally sauntered into the living room a few minutes later, she found Sophie reading through a case file, her pen tapping gently against her teeth in no particular rhythm. Focused and intense, her brow furrowed as she read what looked like a medical report. This was what Rachel loved: the domesticity of their relationship. And yet, they still didn't live together.

"I'm ready," she announced, standing in front of Sophie.

Dark eyes looked up at the sound of the voice and widened. "You look...stunning," Sophie said, pulling herself to her feet. Rachel had her hair up in a simple ponytail. Wispy bits of fringe hung down strategically. She wore a low-cut sleeveless top and a flared skirt with heels that would put her on a par with Sophie's height.

Rachel twirled and let her skirt fly up as she grinned. "Thank you."

"We're going to be late," Sophie mumbled, looking at her watch. Rachel bit her lip and grinned at the sudden change back to serious and surly.

~Grave~

The local Italian restaurant they went to was one of a half dozen in the town centre. Like all of them, it was part of a larger chain, but it did a good meal, and often they got a discount with their phone apps.

The staff knew them well by now too and welcomed Sophie and Rachel in, taking them straight over to the leather booth that was already occupied by Dale and Becky. Each of them had a brightly-coloured drink and a menu in front of them. Whitton wasn't sure why they bothered to look; they always ordered the same thing. Dale would have the American Hot and Becky would go for the Caesar salad, dressing on the side. Then they would order a garlic bread to share and Dale would have onion rings. The drinks were an interesting element to the night's events. Usually Dale had the obligatory one pint, and Becky would have a bottle of wine ready to share with Rachel. Clearly that wasn't going to be the case this evening. Sophie's brain began working through the options and reasons why tonight was different.

"Hey, sorry we're late," Rachel said. She smiled at them both as she took her bag from off her shoulder and slid into the bench on the opposite side of their friends.

Becky smirked. "We actually had a bet going. You're earlier than we expected."

"We're not that bad," Sophie interjected. "Are we?" She laughed and slid in next to Rachel. The blonde's hand moved to instantly rest upon Whitton's thigh. "What's with the funky drinks?"

Dale blushed and looked towards Becky. "It's a mocktail," he mumbled, clearly a little embarrassed to be caught with one, and yet, he had ordered it. Whitton was intrigued further.

"A Mocktail? Right," Whitton teased. "Well, that shirt probably does deserve a little mocking."

"Hey, this is a new shirt." He looked down at the short-sleeve cotton shirt with pink flamingos printed all over it.

"And it's still awful," she replied.

Becky snorted with laughter. "I told him, but he insisted that it was fashion."

The waitress came over and asked about drinks. Rachel pulled up the menu and picked a real cocktail. "I'll have a lemonade, extra ice. Thank you," said Sophie without looking at the menu herself. "So, what gives?" She indicated the drinks again once the waitress had walked away. Becky's mum was babysitting, the same as she did every week when they went out. They usually both had a drink. "You pregnant, Dale?" She laughed at the joke until she noticed the stupid grins on both their faces. "No! Really?"

"Blimey Dale, she is a good detective. Worked it out from one mocktail." Becky grinned.

"Congratulations," Rachel said. "Do the girls know?"

Dale shook his head. "Nah, not yet. We only confirmed it today."

Their drinks arrived and Rachel held hers up to initiate a toast. "To new life," she said. Glasses chinked as they all repeated the words. "It's so exciting."

They placed their orders. Dale had the Hot American, Becky had the salad, and Sophie grinned internally at the normalcy of it all. These were the nights she looked forward to now. The days when a case would get in the way and they'd have to cancel had become the one thing she dreaded. How much things had changed over the last few months.

"So, I uh, didn't get a chance to ask...how your day was?" Sophie spoke quietly to Rachel as she leant in.

"Busy as usual. Sometimes it's like rush hour in Piccadilly Circus in A&E, don't you agree Bec?" Rachel smiled.

Becky nodded and sipped her mocktail. "God yes, and it gets weirder every day. What about that old woman that came in; sat on her knitting needle." She shook her head. "Nasty."

"That does sound painful," Sophie replied, twisting her fork into her linguine.

"Not as painful as that poor kid though. Did you hear about that one?" Becky asked Rachel. Rachel was still chewing on her piece of pizza, something with a lot of chilies on it. Sophie had no intention of sharing that.

"Which one? We have so many," Rachel teased.

"Ain't that the truth!" Becky answered with a giggle. Dale and Sophie exchanged eye rolls and grins. "The blonde kid - I say kid, he is in his twenties easily. Came in after falling off a ladder. Tim said it was bloody lucky, they could easily have missed it."

Everyone turned their attention to her.

"Missed what?" Sophie inquired.

Becky grinned. "Gangrene. Apparently, he's been injecting between his toes. Of course, it was a fall so nobody was going to look at his feet, but they had to strip him off obviously. Gonna lose the toe, that's for sure."

"Blimey." Dale muttered as he took another mouthful.

Nurses and police officers sharing a macabre sense of humour and an interest in the gorier details was pretty much the way of it, and nobody would be put off their food.

"So, are you two allowed to say what case you're working on?" Becky asked once their main meal was finished. Dale looked towards Sophie for confirmation that he could share the details. She shrugged and nodded.

"Well," he said, wasting no time. "We've got a strange one, actually."

Rachel leant her chin on the bridge of her hands and listened intently. Sophie hadn't been forthcoming at home about her own work. She would sit and read her files quietly, but she rarely talked about her cases lately.

"How strange?" Rachel teased. "Does it beat the woman that managed to lose a can of deodorant up her..."

"Rachel!" Becky laughed.

Dale blushed. "Uh, no, probably not that strange." He laughed. "You've read in the paper about the grave murders, right?" He sat up straighter as he spoke. "We think we're dealing with a vigilante."

"Really?" Rachel asked. She always got more information out of Dale than she did Sophie.

Sophie interjected. "They do all seem to be connected."

The waitress reappeared. "All okay? Can I get anyone any more drinks? Would you like to see the dessert menu?" she rambled off quickly before they had a chance to answer any of her questions.

"Uh, yes it was lovely, thank you," Sophie answered for them. "Do you want anything else?" She asked the group.

"Yes, I want to hear the end of this. I'll have a coffee and the dessert menu, please." Rachel grinned.

Following a brief discussion, Dale and Becky both ordered further mocktails. With desserts ordered, Dale then filled them in on all the details he and Sophie were prepared to give.

Chapter Twenty-Two

The pub wasn't that busy. It was a weekday, so most people were at work, but that didn't seem to have any impact on the few occupants inside who clearly didn't see the need for employment, and who shouted more loudly the drunker they got. The summer sun brought them all outside. Luckily for him, that meant that inside was virtually empty; just the way he wanted it.

He stood beneath a grand oak opposite the building, covered by the greenery of low branches as he leant against the trunk and observed those lurking in the beer garden. The guilty one was laughing and clowning around with his friends; not a care in the world. He held a pint in his hand that slopped about with his movements, spilling over the rim of the glass while his friends got rowdier. A girl pushed him away and the crowd of men jeered and laughed as she got in his face and told him in no uncertain terms not to touch her again.

And then his chance appeared. The kid swallowed down the rest of his beer and scrunched the plastic cup in his hand before flinging it at his friend. He leant in and said something that earned another raucous cackle before wandering inside, alone.

This was his moment. The chance he had known would come if he was just patient enough.

Stepping out from the shadow of the tree, he made his way across the pub carpark and inside the building unseen. Nobody paid any attention to a workman going about his business. The men's toilet was tucked away in the corner; out of sight and away from the CCTV that covered the main bar.

Opening the bag, he pulled out the *Closed for cleaning* sign and set it in front of the door. He brazenly then held the door for a man as he came out, still zipping his fly.

"Thanks," he muttered, paying no attention to his helper.

Now he smiled; he was invisible.

The small room stank of piss. The floor was wet with what he already knew would be a mixture of urine and alcohol. The short figure of Trevor Hayes stood in front of the urinal, left hand placed against the wall as he held himself upright. His cock, held in his right hand, sprayed the wall as he swayed drunkenly left and right.

It felt like a lifetime as he waited for him to finish. His heart beat faster than ever before as he prayed that nobody else would wander in before he had his chance. This was the most brazen he had been. But the pub was quiet now; nearly everyone had left.

Hayes looked up and noticed his reflection in the shiny metal that covered the wall. He turned slightly. "What you looking at? Fucking perv." He turned and faced him. "You want some of this, do ya?" he said, wagging his penis at him and laughing. "Go on then, on ya knees. Suck it."

A grin appeared on the man's face that made Hayes look twice. Hayes didn't expect him to move forward and take him up on the offer. "I have something for you," he said. Hayes' eyes narrowed.

"Fuck off, bloody faggot." Tucking himself away and zipping his fly, he laughed in the man's face as he passed him. He wasn't laughing when he felt the prick to his neck and the woozy feeling that came over him in an instant.

The man grabbed him as he slumped to the floor, lifting him up and tucking his arm under Trevor's and around his waist. Just another guy helping his drunken friend home.

He was sweating by the time he got him back to the car and pushed Hayes into the boot. But that didn't matter. A quick glance around and he stripped off the boiler suit and pushed it into the black plastic bag he kept in the boot, along with the wig and gloves. All of it would burn. He grabbed a new suit and pulled that on.

Climbing into the car, he caught his reflection in the mirror and smiled to himself, satisfied that once more, he had set the record straight. Now, all that was left to do was to drop off the body and let the world see that justice had been served.

He checked his watch. Darren Barton's funeral had finished an hour ago. Perfect timing.

~Grave~

The church was deserted; nobody would be coming now. He parked as close as he dared and pulled the trolley out of the boot. It was one of those collapsible ones that folded almost flat but could carry upwards of 200 pounds, and it was big enough to drag Trevor Hayes' unconscious body from the back of the car and sit him in it. A couple of bungee ties held Hayes' back upright against the handles as the trolley tilted back and he pulled it across the grass.

The grave site was still covered in beautiful floral wreaths, and he carefully moved them out of the way, leaning them up against others around the newly dug ground. It was a beautiful spot really, one that Darren Barton would never get to enjoy.

It took a while for Hayes to come around. A little longer than he had expected, given the dose. He had prepared well, guessing him to be just shy of five feet, six inches and weighing no more than 130 pounds. But clearly, the alcohol had interacted with the drug, and he had to resort to slapping his face to bring him around enough to understand what was happening.

It happened fast. A glint of something shiny and then Hayes screamed as something stabbed at him. Blood sprayed much like his piss had done earlier, and he fell to the floor, clutching his groin.

"Why? I didn't do nuffin to you," Hayes sniffed, his eyes pleading for help.

He didn't speak, just turned his head to face the grave and watched as comprehension moved into place.

"I didn't…" He was almost there. Consciousness was slipping from his grasp, this time from the sudden drop of blood pressure.

A blank stare and then it was done.

Chapter Twenty-Three

DS Dale Saint had prepared well. On Whitton's desk was a take-away cup of coffee and a salted caramel muffin from her favourite coffee shop. She raised a brow as the files she carried dropped onto the desk next to them. The main office had been quiet as she strode through, but she had spotted him at his desk. It was obvious that it was him who had brought the refreshments. Picking up the cup, she took a tentative sip; still hot. She winced at the heat of it hitting her tongue. Taking a seat, she noticed the envelope with her name scrawled across it in Dale's handwriting. She smirked to herself, knowing there was more to it than just a nice gesture. He was buttering her up for something.

She picked it up and spun it, corner to corner, between her fingers. It wasn't the usual brown office envelope. This one was an expensive white one with tiny little embossed flowers around the edge. Something Becky would have chosen for sure.

Her finger slid underneath the flap and pried it open, withdrawing a single sheet of paper that matched the envelope.

Dear Sophie,

There are times in life when you must pick out the people that will be there should the worst happen, for us, that is you. I know that you're not the religious type, but we are. We go to church as often as we can and both Harry and Ella were christened, just as we plan to do so with this new life. Becky and I would be honoured if you would act as Godmother to our next child.

Dale & Becky.

She reread the note again. Being responsible for a child was a huge commitment to take on should the unfortunate situation arise, and a decision she wouldn't take lightly. Her eyes closed and she found herself transported back to the previous year when her then-girlfriend, Yvonne, had wanted a child, a child she too had thought she wanted. But things hadn't worked out that way.

"You read it then?" Dale's voice brought her from her thoughts. He stood in the door, leaning against the frame, fiddling with his ring.

She nodded. "I did, yes." She picked up the coffee cup and pulled off the plastic lid to sip it.

"So?"

"I'll think about. It's not something to take lightly…it's…it's an honour, Dale. Thank you for thinking of me."

He grinned at her, fully expecting her reaction. "Well, we talked about it, and both of us agreed we wanted you."

Before she could answer, the phone rang. Snatching it up, she growled into the handset, "Whitton."

~Grave~

Gina Ashcroft screamed down the phone line and into Whitton's ear. She was making no sense. Saint could hear the noise from three feet away and turned towards her, concerned.

"Gina, calm down, okay? I can't..." She pulled the phone away from her ear as another torrent of high-pitched screeching came at her. "Gina!" she shouted louder, and for a second there was an intake of breath, but that soon turned into sobs.

"Who would do such a thing?" Whitton finally understood something she said. Gina continued to wail.

She perched on the corner of her desk and held the phone back to her ear. "Gina, take a deep breath and explain to me what exactly has you all upset like this."

"Yesterday was Darren's...funeral." The wailing began again, and it took all of Whitton's self-control not to roll her eyes. "Someone...on his, someone died and it's not fair."

"No, I know. Darren's death was..."

"No!" Gina screamed. "You don't understand, not Darren. Someone else. Someone else is dead...on Darren's grave!"

~Grave~

Dale Saint struggled to keep up with Whitton. She all but marched from the car before it finished screeching to a halt. The office had gone haywire once Whitton understood what it was that Gina was telling her. Saint, Bowen, and Branson were all on her tail as she flew out the door, shouting instructions to them. Barnard was called and was on his way but right now, they needed to secure the area.

"It's Trevor Hayes," Branson confirmed from a quick glance. "Fucking blood everywhere."

"Right, everyone back up till the Scenes of Crime lot get here," Saint instructed.

"This is downright under our noses," Bowen complained as they stood a few feet from the body. Uniform officers were already putting up a cordon and blocking entrance to anyone trying to enter the cemetery. "How did he get here and do this? The funeral was only yesterday."

Whitton remained silent. Hayes' body lay on top of the grave. The flowers that would have been there had been moved to one side, that much was obvious, but she would get confirmation from Gina.

She swiveled on her heels and located the woman. Head to toe in black, she dabbed at her makeup-smeared face with a tissue. PC Watson looked as bored as hell while he stood next to her, attempting to be sympathetic and doing a reasonably good job of it.

Whitton listened; eyes closed. Chattering coppers filtered out as sounds around her took centre stage: birds twittering in the breeze. The sound of three vehicles pulling in one after the other onto the gravel and parking, doors opening and slamming shut, alerted her. Barnard had arrived.

She waited.

The giant of a man stood beside her and appraised the scene too. "Well, isn't this fun?" he said, the hint of a smile on his lips. "He isn't wasting any time, is he?"

"No. Let's hope his eagerness left something behind."

Dr. Tristan Barnard set to work, clambering into his oversized coverall while he ordered his technicians to do the tasks that needed doing. They began to sweep the perimeter, checking for any clue that might have been left behind, no matter how minuscule it might be.

He passed Whitton a coverall and waited until she was clad like he was, complete with white booties and a blue material hat. "Let me guess, stab wound to the thigh?"

"Better be careful, Doc. They'll all be wanting the lottery results if you prove to be psychic." She smirked and squatted down to look at the wound while she pulled latex gloves on her bony fingers.

"Single stab wound to the left thigh," he said, poking the area with a gloved finger. "What's remarkable is that it's a direct hit. No other attempt to stab him, just the artery. That says to me that we could be looking for someone with a medical background or at the very least a good knowledge of anatomy."

"Alright."

"And somebody physically strong." He looked the body up and down. "Trevor Hayes wasn't a heavy guy but still, it would take some doing to force him here."

She looked back over her shoulder towards the car park. It wasn't a huge cemetery, but newer graves were towards the back. It was certainly a distance. She stood up and looked to the ground. Footprints were few in the dried earth and grass. The hard-baked soil held just remnants of scuff marks, mostly from their own feet and those of Darren Barton's mourners. But something caught her eye in the short, patchy grass. There was an indent into the ground and another parallel to it. Head and shoulders bent forward, she moved slowly and found another. Just the one this time, in a shallow dip.

"Nobody moves," she called out, reaching for a marker and placing it down next to the three marks. Barnard stood up and held his hand up, indicating that his staff remain still. "He uses something with wheels. Here and here..." She pointed down to the floor. "Indents of wheels carrying something heavy." She turned back and moved her hand back and forth where it was more earth than grass. "He's brushed them away here, it's too clean. This area should be covered in footprints from the mourners, but it's not." Now she moved forward, following the direction of the lines. Stopping each time, she picked up the trail and marked it. Within a few minutes they knew the path he had taken and where the car must have been parked. The gravel had been ground down and flushed away over the years to leave a sandy base exposed and in it, the perfect print of a tyre.

"Not that fucking smart, are you?" she said to herself as she waved over the tech nearest to her. "Get a mould and photographs of that." As she turned to walk away, she threw a quick "Thanks" over her shoulder at Barry before looking around for Tweedle Dee. Perkins wasn't here to letch over her, thankfully.

Ducking back under the cordon to head to her car, she saw a group of journalists closing in. Reporters from local newspapers and TV stations were all shouting questions at her as she passed.

"DI Whitton, have we got another Doll Maker?!" the nearest one to her shouted. When she ignored him, he continued. "Whitton, when ya gonna put a stop to this?"

She didn't miss a step. She was used to the press hounding for details at a crime scene.

"Come on Whitton, you're not fucking this one's sister too, are ya?" someone from the back shouted.

"Fuck off," she snarled, twisting round to see who said it. The voice disappeared into the throng. Saint touched her arm and guided her away.

"Ignore him."

Chapter Twenty-Four

Sitting inside the chief's office, Whitton waited quietly while he finished a call. She thought she knew what was coming. When he finally placed the handset back down into its cradle and looked up, she was sure of it.

"I want you and Saint to do a press conference. See if we can get a heads up on this with the public."

"Yes, sir." She sighed. She hated these. She didn't want to be the public face of anything, and she especially didn't want to deal with journalists who would just sensationalise everything.

"Everything's arranged. Local hacks and TV will be here in an hour. Have a statement prepared, and let's see if we can finally get something on this so-called Judge and Jury."

Nodding, she stood and walked towards the door.

"By the way Whitton, how are things now, with..." he probed gently. The mental health of his best detective was important to him.

"I'm feeling much better, Sir. Dr. Westbrook is...well, I'm working through some things still, but..."

This time it was him that nodded, his cheeks reddening a little. "Good, good. Keep it up."

~Grave~

Whitton sat next to Saint behind a long table in a small room with an abundance of lenses looking back at them. Four microphones sat on the desk in front of them, and flashbulbs intermittently went off, blinding them both for a moment.

"Good afternoon, ladies and gentlemen. Thank you all for attending today," she began. *Be nice; keep them sweet.* "We would like to ask the public for any help they might be able to give. As you may be aware, we are involved in an ongoing investigation into the death of Anita Simmons. We are now linking that death to that of Trevor Hayes, whose body was found most recently. We have also managed to link the deaths of George Herring and Paul Crawford. Both of those deaths are historical but still open cases."

The bulbs flashed with more intensity now. She took the opportunity to sip some water.

"We would like to speak to anyone who may have any information regarding these deaths. We can be contacted here, at Woodington Police Station. A number has been set up especially for this case and details will, I am advised, appear on the screen."

"Detective, is this a new Doll Maker?" the voice called out from the back, and Whitton spotted the same guy from the cemetery.

"No, we do not believe that the person responsible for these deaths is a serial killer."

"And yet, they've killed at least four people. Surely one more and they officially become a serial killer? Is Woodington safe?"

This time it was Dale who spoke. "Woodington is very safe. Otherwise I wouldn't live here with my family."

"Is it true that DI Whitton's partner is the sister of the Doll Maker?"

Whitton's eyes scanned the crowd and found the face. A sly grin stared back at her. She recognised him; one of the local journos whose nickname among the ranks was Gutter Gob.

"DI Whitton isn't here to discuss her private life. Nor are you," Saint threw back. "If that's all." He stood and waited for Whitton to join him. "Just ignore it," he whispered as he leant in to her.

"Getting sick and fucking tired of him asking that question."

They left the cameras behind them and exited the room. "I know. It's Gutter Gob, he couldn't find a story if we wrote it for him. He just likes to fuck with us."

She ran a hand through her hair. "Yeah, you're right."

~Grave~

Barry waved at them as they parked the car outside of the pathology block. He was heading out and carrying medical bags and supplies for the van. "What is his name?" Whitton asked as she nodded an acknowledgement. If he expected a smile, he was sadly disappointed.

"Barry?"

"Yeah, I meant his surname. I can't keep calling him Tweedle Dum. One day I'm going to say it out loud." She climbed out of the car and adjusted her shirt; it was sticking to her in the heat.

Dale chuckled. "I think it's Walker, but I might be wrong. To be honest, I don't really care," he said, pushing his sunglasses back up his nose. "He's a knob."

She nodded. "Me either, but I should at least appear to be bothered by such things. I might have to write him into my report, and then what do I say? 'On March 12, Tweedle Dum and Tweedle Dee arrived on scene to collect the remains of...'" She laughed, and so did Dale. "Where is Tweedle Dee anyway, don't they usually end up working the same shifts? I don't think I've seen them apart more than a handful of times."

"You spoke too soon," Dale said, jutting his chin forwards and towards the approaching figure of Dr. Clive Perkins. His step seemed to quicken at the sight of them, and a grin appeared.

Whitton groaned. "Miss your ride? He just left," she said loudly in his direction.

"Ah, yes. That's because I have somewhere else that I need to be," he said, coming to a stop in front of them. His eyes roamed Whitton's chest again. "Nice to see you though, DI Whitton."

She felt her skin crawl. Maybe it was the heat, or the injustice that three people were on her murder board, or maybe she just didn't like him, but without a thought her palm thrust forward and pushed him hard in the chest. Launching him against a car, she pressed hard and leaned in close. "Maybe if you didn't stare at my tits every time I met you, it would be nice for me too."

Dale's eyes widened and he choked back a laugh, but he didn't intervene.

"I...that's..." Perkins stammered, and she enjoyed it, making him squirm for a change. She glared a moment longer before releasing her grip and taking a step back.

"I'm not that tall that your line of sight can't move a few inches upwards. Am I clear?"

He made a noise that sounded like a harrumph and walked away quickly, his cheeks blushing a deep red.

"Yeah, I think he got the message, don't you?"

Now Dale chuckled. "If he didn't, he's a fool."

"Come on, let's see what the doc has to say about Trevor Haye's autopsy report."

~Grave~

Tristan Barnard stood to his full height at the window in his office, looking down at the car park. He witnessed the altercation between Whitton and Perkins, and grinned. It was about time someone dealt with the irritating man, but the fact that it was DI Sophie Whitton somewhat aroused him. He continued to stare out across the car park until he heard the light knock on his door announcing Whitton's arrival.

"Detectives, what brings you here?" He smiled, the corners of his eyes crinkling. "Other than to assault a member of my staff."

Whitton titled her head at him. "Don't know what you're talking about. Did you see anyone assaulted, Dale?" she asked, turning her attention to her partner.

He shook his head. "Nope. I did witness sexual harassment though, is that what you meant?" His smiling eyes landed on the doctor.

"Tea?" He didn't wait for a reply before he began the ritual of making a pot. "I suppose you want to know about Trevor Hayes?"

"Yes," she said, taking a seat. Saint followed. "Tell me you found something, anything!"

He poured the boiling water over the leaves and then stirred gently. "I can tell you that he was injected with ketamine. It's a sedative and would have rendered him unconscious or at the very least, extremely pliable!"

Saint sat forwards. "That will explain how he managed to get him to the cemetery then."

"Indeed. We also found an oily substance much like the one found on Anita Simmons. I should have the results back on that any time," Tristan said, bringing the pot to the table. "And we found blue fibers."

Chapter Twenty-Five

Dr. Westbrook was still with a client when Whitton arrived for her next appointment the following afternoon. She chewed on the inside of her mouth as her leg bounced on a nerve. This was the worst bit, the waiting around. Westbrook always overran. She considered just arriving 5 minutes after her scheduled time, but being late wasn't in her nature unless it was unavoidable. Or maybe she just used that as her excuse when she wanted to avoid something. Her ex, Yvonne, would agree with that.

The door opened and a dark-haired man in his twenties shuffled out, head bowed and hands in his pockets. He looked like the kind of person she arrested, but she said nothing and examined her fingernails instead.

"Ms. Whitton, you can go in now." The soft voice of Anne broke her from her thoughts. She smiled at the older woman on reception and got up, blowing out a breath of hot air in the process.

It was cool inside the office. A glass of water sat on the coaster as usual, ready for her to drink when her mouth dried up and her throat constricted with emotion.

"Good afternoon, Sophie. How are you today?"

"I'm good," she said, reaching for the glass. She took a small swig, placed it back down on the coaster, and wiped the condensation from her hand onto her leg.

Dr. Westbrook leant back in her seat. She had one of those expensive ergonomic leather chairs that tilted, and she rocked gently in it as she composed her next question. Sophie stretched out a leg and yawned. "Not sleeping?"

"I sleep fine, mostly. Last night was a late night, that's all."

Dr. Westbrook smiled. "That's good. Anything you want to tell me?"

Sophie narrowed her eyes at her. She was never quite sure how she did that, how she knew when Sophie had something specific she wanted to talk about. She ran her fingers through her hair and leant back. Her chair didn't recline unless she pulled the lever. "I talked with Rachel about you and the flashbacks."

"That's good, that's progress, Sophie."

She nodded and bit her bottom lip. "I think I scared her; I know that I scared me."

"Go on," Dr. Westbrook encouraged, and Sophie felt almost compelled to just spill it all. But then she remembered what she would need to tell, and it embarrassed her. It made her feel awkward. "I'm not here to judge, Sophie," Westbrook reminded her.

"Fuck," Whitton mumbled as she pulled herself up and onto her feet. She paced the room, running her hand's through her hair again. When she came to a halt in front of the window, she looked out at the blue sky. Barely any clouds, just a blue expanse.

"It isn't even that recent, I don't even know how many days ago. I just can't get past it. I can't even…sometimes she wants me to…" She rubbed her face in her hands, searching for the right words that would explain it, but nothing poetic seemed to come. "She likes things a bit rough…in bed," she finally forced out. "She likes me to be…she says there are two of me." Turning back to face the doctor, she wrapped her arms around herself as she fought with her own mind what to say and how to explain it.

"There's Sophie who makes love to her, respects her, and cherishes everything about her." Closing her eyes, she took a slow, deep breath. "And then there is Whitton. Forceful, unashamed and unrelenting. And she likes it, I know that, but this was different." She rubbed her neck and stared back out of the window as an elderly couple slowly walked down the road, hands joined between them, the outer hands holding onto walking sticks. "I had this need to consume her. To be inside her and…I was relentless. I just kept thrusting and thrusting. It wasn't…I didn't feel anything; it was like I was numb to it."

"What did Rachel say about it?"

Sophie turned to face her again. "She asked me what brought that on? So, I told her."

"What did you tell her?"

"That I needed to feel her...alive."

"And did she understand what you meant by that?"

Whitton nodded.

She walked back across the room and sat down again in the chair. Closing her eyes, she tried to remember the conversation. "She said I could fuck her like that anytime, she wasn't complaining. And then she said that she wanted to move in with me."

"And how do you feel about that?"

"I actually really want to...but not before I can control this anger."

"Have you made love since?"

"Love? That wasn't love!" Sophie shook her head, anger rising to the surface. "I love her so much but that, that wasn't...if she hadn't stopped me, I don't know what I'd have done, how far I'd have pushed."

Dr. Westbrook considered that. "Have you been intimate since?" she tried again.

Sophie nodded. "Yes."

"And on that occasion, was it making love?"

Again, Sophie nodded. "Yes, that was when I told her about you and seeing her at crime scenes."

"And what did she say to that?"

"She was happy that I told her."

"Using sex as a way to communicate isn't uncommon." Dr. Westbrook smiled and sat forward. "The problem is that you're not communicating how you feel. Sophie, you're suffering from PTSD. It's perfectly normal for you to feel the way you do, and we're going to find ways for you to deal with it. Opening up to Rachel about seeing me and your flashbacks, that's a good start."

"I know, it's just frustrating, you know? Yesterday I..."

"Go on."

"I got really angry, like it just surged up and before I knew it, I had a colleague almost by the throat."

"What had he done to cause that anger?"

Sophie crossed her arms again. "He's just a perv, always staring at my..." She looked down at her breasts. "It's not like I haven't dealt with that kind of shit before, but with him...he just reminds me..." Her words drifted off as realisation hit home.

Westbrook waited a moment and then pushed. "He reminds you of..."

"Anthony, it's how Anthony looked at me." She looked up into the eyes of her doctor. "What do I do?"

"I think that you need to carry on what you have started. Talk to Rachel, Sophie. Explain everything, let her talk to you. I have no doubt she is probably suffering from PTSD herself. Is she getting any counselling?"

Sophie shook her head. "She didn't want it."

"Well, as I say, there are things that you both need to talk to each other about. I want you to try something."

"Fine."

"When Rachel spends the night next, I want you to play a game." Whitton rolled her eyes. "Don't worry, I think you'll like this. The rules are very simple. You can only undress each other if you have answered the question."

"What question?"

"Whatever question the other wishes to ask."

"Let me get this straight. You want us to get into bed fully clothed and ask each other questions, to which an answer will win the person the right to remove an article of clothing?"

Westbrook smiled across the desk. "That's the rules. Intimacy and learning to talk to one another. Oh, and did I mention, you can't have sex?"

~Grave~

"What are you looking for?" Dale asked, finding Whitton in her office on the computer watching grainy CCTV.

Without turning away from the screen, she mumbled, "Anything." He remained silent and she looked up at him. "Anything from the news conference?"

"Other than the usual nutters with nothing of interest? No."

Jeff had put together a video containing all the CCTV recordings of Anita Simmons and her potential whereabouts on the day she died. It was always a bit weird watching a dead person going about their business, unaware of what was to come. Grabbing a chair, Dale pulled it up beside her and plonked himself down. "Where'd you go earlier?"

"Out."

"Obviously." They both stared at the screen and watched as the general public went about its business. "Where?"

"Dale, back off, alright?" Her voice stayed low, mindful of the others outside of the room. "I had an appointment; I've been and now I am back."

He held his hands up. "Fine, I was just concerned. You've disappeared a few times lately, and..."

"Fuck's sake, do I need permission from you? Last time I looked I was your superior." She stood up, knocking her chair flying. "I am going home now, that okay with you?"

"Soph, come on...that's not..." But she was gone. The rest of the room was silent. "...what I meant," he finished under his breath, picking the chair up and sliding it back under the desk. The low hum of voices murmuring filled the quiet, and he flopped down into his chair and resumed watching the video.

~Grave~

Rachel pottered about the kitchen. She wanted to make sure that dinner would be ready for Sophie, whatever time she got home. It was just gone four p.m., so she wasn't expecting her for a while. The radio was on, pumping out old school tunes, and Rachel found herself singing along.

She had a leg of lamb slow roasting in the oven; Sophie's favourite. The smell was delicious as it wafted through the tiny cottage. These were the days she hated most: being alone in the house. She kept herself busy and tried to keep her thoughts away from that awful event that almost took her life.

When the doorbell rang, she instinctively flinched as memories of Anthony flooded her mind. Composing herself, she wiped her hands on a tea towel as she walked towards the door. Her lips curled at the edges as she heard Sophie's key in the door. She had been doing that for a while now, always ringing the bell first after coming in one night and scaring the hell out of her.

"Hey, what brings you here so early?" Rachel said, reaching out for her hand. Sophie let her take it. Dropping her satchel down on the floor, she kicked off one shoe and then the other.

"I just needed you," she replied honestly, wrapping her arms around her girlfriend.

"Not that I am unhappy about that; in fact, I really like it, but are you okay?" Rachel asked, pulling back from her. There were times with Sophie where Rachel thought maybe she needed more from her.

"Yes. No." She sighed and sat down on the couch, pulling Rachel to sit on her lap. "I saw Dr. Westbrook today."

"Okay."

Her head fell back against the sofa, and Rachel brushed her hand through Sophie's hair and around her ear to rest her palm on Sophie's cheek. "I have homework," Sophie admitted.

Rachel pressed her lips to her neck and let them rest there, enjoying this closeness. She snuggled in and Sophie took her hand. Soft, gentle hands, Sophie thought.

"I want to live with you. I love you and I want that with you."

"I feel a really big 'but' coming," Rachel said quietly.

"Yeah. I think before we can consider it, we both need to sort ourselves out."

Rachel sat up quickly, her eyes narrowing. "What do you mean?"

"Come on, Rach."

"No, I'm fine." She looked away.

Sophie exhaled and licked at her lips. "Okay, well I'm not." She shook her head and frowned. "I'm not dealing with it well and I wanna fix it; fix me. I don't want to make the same mistakes I did with Yvonne."

For a moment there was silence. Sophie thought that Rachel might even be ignoring her, but then just as Sophie was about to speak again, Rachel spoke.

"What's the homework?"

Sophie pinched the bridge of her nose, a thin-lipped smile appearing. "I told her about the other night." At Rachel's confused look, she continued. "How I got too rough with you."

"I didn't say you were too rough."

"No, but that's how I feel about it; I wasn't in control." She shook her head at herself, the darkness she lived in falling all around her. "I don't want you to become something I use when I lose control."

"Babe, I know you wouldn't do that."

"But I did, that's what I did Rach. I felt like the only way that I could really feel you…the only way I could fully know that you were alive was to…was to dominate you like that, and I don't like it."

Rachel thought about it, thought about herself and how she reacted to things now. She had just put it down to a normal reaction to what happened, but now she reconsidered. Was it normal to jump any time someone walked past her too closely and she hadn't seen them? Was it normal for her to hate being alone in the house, but feel completely safe when she was alone at Sophie's place? "What do we do?"

"Just this, we talk about it. We talk about everything that bothers us."

"That's it?"

Sophie smirked. "We uh, well Westbrook says we can't...we can't have sex."

Rachel's eyes widened. "What? Is she serious?"

Sophie nodded; she already knew this wouldn't be something that Rachel would like. "She suggests that we learn to be intimate together but without the sex. The idea is that we spend time together, fully clothed, and we talk, we ask questions, and with every answer, we can remove an item of clothing. We can cuddle and kiss, but that's it. The point is that we learn to communicate in a way that doesn't involve sex."

Sophie remained silent and waited for Rachel's reaction. Her breathing felt calm, and she was quietly impressed with how relaxed she felt just getting this off her chest. She would have to apologise to Dale in the morning. The way she had reacted was not how she wanted to behave with her friend.

"If we do this...can I move into your place?" Rachel's voice sounded small and scared.

"If you still want to."

Rachel nodded.

Chapter Twenty-Six

It was foggy the following morning. Mist off the sea 40 miles away had rolled in and would linger until the heat of the sun burned its way through. Whitton arrived at the station early with iced coffees and a bag of muffins. She felt rested after the previous night. They'd gone to bed and continued to talk. The conversation was light, but it was better than the silent brooding that would begin and put an end to any sexual activity since The Doll Maker case.

The office was empty this early as she placed a coffee down on Dale's desk, the condensation dripping down the plastic cup, already forming a ring of water around it. Inside her office, she found a note stuck to her computer screen written in Dale's messy scrawl.

Fast forward to 13:24. Dale.

Sucking cold coffee through the straw, she booted up the computer and felt that ripple of goosebumps marching up her arm in anticipation of finding a lead. The screen jumped to life, lighting up her face in the darkened room. When she heard the sharp knock, she looked up and found Dale in the doorway. "Safe to come in, I assume?" He grinned, holding up a peace offering: a chocolate muffin in a paper bag.

"Yeah, sorry. I just have stuff going on." She indicated a chair. "Shut the door."

He did as he was asked and pulled the chair out, sitting down gently. "You okay?" His concern warmed her, but that didn't mean she found it easy to confide.

Sitting back in her chair, she contemplated how much to tell him, deciding her usual blunt self would probably be best. "I'm seeing a counsellor."

Nodding, he said, "Okay."

"Unsurprisingly, I've got PTSD."

He nodded again. "Okay." He took a sip of his drink. "If you need me to cover for you, just gimme the nod, alright?"

"Thanks." Thin lips pressed out a smile. "So, what did you find?" she said, jutting her chin towards the screen that was now alive and waiting for instructions.

"I'm not sure, but at some point, Anita stops and talks to someone offscreen." The video sped along through time as Whitton fast forwarded to the relevant point. "Look, right there. She stops and turns to her left. She's sideways so it's hard to make out what she is saying, but there is a conversation and it's heated, but then she walks in that direction." They watched as Anita Simmons turned left and right as though she were trying to decide something.

"It's a car, right? That's the front wing of a black car," Whitton said, pointing to the screen.

"Yeah, but watch." Anita Simmons then stepped out into the road and went off screen. The car didn't move. They watched for five more minutes, and it stayed stationary.

"Where has she gone?"

"Dunno, but whoever she spoke to knows." He slurped the last of his drink and tossed the cup into the recycle bin. "That's Markham St, I thought we could go down there and see if anyone remembers anything?"

~Grave~

Markham St was full of the kind of shops Whitton's mother would call exotic. There was the Polish market and the Indian shop that sold every spice and ingredient you could think of. The powerful smell of curry powder, garlic, and coriander wafted out and transported you to the streets of Delhi. Whitton wasn't much of a cook, but Rachel had dragged her down here a few times when she had found a recipe she wanted to try. Turkish, Iranian, and Italian delicatessens, and even a Chinese wholesaler could be found open to the public. It was outside of the Chinese place that Whitton and Saint worked out Anita had been standing. The black car was parked in the same spot.

"So, where do you want to start?" Whitton looked across the road at the derelict sight. Builder's boards surrounded what had once been a row of shops, now being knocked down for a luxury block of flats.

"I guess we start in here?" Dale hooked a thumb over his shoulder at the wholesaler's. A member of staff sat at the till directly in front of the window and would have had a good view of the area at any time of day.

She pushed open the door and made her way around 10 kilogram bags of rice piled up in the middle of the aisle. A teenage girl sat idly at the till on her phone. The place wasn't busy. It looked rundown and ramshackle, but that wasn't Whitton's concern.

She held up her warrant card at the girl. Wide eyes now looked from the phone to the ID and then to Whitton and Saint. "Hi, DI Whitton and this is DS Saint, we were hoping we could talk to whoever was working the till on Monday."

"That was me," the girl said nervously, pushing her glasses up her nose. "I work the day shifts Monday through till Friday."

"Right, and your name is?"

"Nian Zang Chen." Dale wrote it down. "Am I in trouble?"

"No, we were just wondering if you noticed anything out of the ordinary?"

The girl put her phone down on the till and considered it. "I mean, you've seen what it's like around here, right? There is a lot of odd stuff happening."

"We're interested in something that happened around one o'clock. Two or more people having a heated discussion?" Dale mentioned.

Whitton smiled kindly and reached into her pocket. "Did you notice this woman?"

Nian took the photo and studied it. "I think so, it's hard to tell because the woman that was shouting had her back to me." She handed back the photograph of Anita Simmons.

"Okay, did you see who she was shouting at?"

She nodded slowly. "It was a white guy, old, maybe like…fifties?"

Dale felt the hair prickle in the back of his neck. "Anything else?"

"He looked out of place, ya know? Like he really doesn't work in overalls." She shrugged. "He was standing over there." She pointed to the opposite side of the road where there was a large tree. "I think he knew her; he was waving and she stopped, turned towards him and shouted something, but I couldn't hear what it was. Then he beckoned her over, like this." She used her right hand to bend her fingers back and forth. "She wasn't having it though, but they chatted for a bit and she left smiling. He went the other way."

Whitton looked at Dale. "The one direction we have no CCTV for?"

"He's smart." He turned back to Nian. "Do you think you'd be able to describe him to an artist?"

"I'll give it a go."

Chapter Twenty-Seven

"You know what I don't get?" Dale said, sitting back in his chair and raising his arms behind his head. Sophie looked up from her file and placed her pen down on the desk. She waited expectantly. "No forensics. Nothing, nada, zilch. How can that be?"

"People are savvier nowadays I suppose. They know what we are looking for. They know how to cover themselves."

"So, wouldn't that person stand out more? If they're all wrapped up, in this weather?"

Something about that triggered a thought in Whitton. "Hold on, put that video back on." Dale loaded up the file and waited for it to buffer. "I'm sure there was..." The scene on the screen showed Anita Simmons leaving the store. "Fast forward a bit."

They watched the world speed up, legs moving faster than would usually be the case as people went about their daily business, unaware of the drama that was unfolding around them. Anita moved into another shop, laughing and smiling with someone as she left. "There." Whitton pointed. "Right there, who is that?"

The screen filled with the image of a man, a tall, stocky man in blue overalls like a builder would wear. He wore a cap pulled down over his face. "Looks like a workman," Dale offered. "Nian said he wore overalls."

"There isn't a mark on him. Anytime I have met anyone wearing that getup, they have been covered in paint, oil, dust...They don't buy new ones each time they have a new job."

"True." Dale made a print of the image and then hit fast-forward again. Anita continued with her journey. She stopped to speak with a woman who warmly rubbed Anita's arm with her palm. They were smiling at one another and chatted for several minutes. Nothing about it suggested alarm. Dale stopped the tape. "There." He pointed to the background of the image. A grainy figure in blue, wearing a cap, stood watching.

Whitton felt the hairs stand up on her arms. "Keep going."

Dale pressed fast-forward again. The images skipped here and there where CCTV was lost and then picked up elsewhere. She was about halfway between leaving the last store and where she had disappeared.

"Shit, look, right there." The man was right behind Anita as she came into view. "It can't be coincidence. He is following her."

"Looks like it, and his appearance fits with Nian's description."

"Keep looking, print off as many images as you can. Maybe we will get lucky," she said grabbing her bag.

"Where you going?"

"Barnard, I wanna check in and keep him up-to-date."

~Grave~

Once again Whitton found no parking space outside of the lab. She drove around the block and swore under her breath as every space was snatched up before she could get there. She swung the car left, intent on going around again, and got stuck behind an ambulance as it unloaded a patient. She put the car into park and waited, her window wound down to allow a slight breeze to flow inside at least. Glancing to her left, she saw Perkins and his team heading out. They would be freeing up a space.

Finally, the ambulance moved. She swung the car back around and headed for Perkins' spot. He was sitting inside the vehicle faffing around with paperwork. He glanced up quickly and noticed her waiting, but did nothing to speed up his process. She gave him a quick bib of the horn and a thumbs up to indicate that she wanted his space. His response was to wave back, grinning inanely at her.

"For fuck's sake," she muttered and rubbed at her face. A minute later Barry crossed in front of her and jumped in beside Perkins. She couldn't remember his last name, but he was another dick. "Tweedle fucking Dum and Dee," she muttered to herself.

They finally pulled out, and Whitton waved them off before reversing into the space. A loud bang on the side of the car made her jump. Barnard's face grinned in at her.

"Jesus, Tristan." She pushed the door open and almost hit him with it as he roared with laughter. "You're a shit."

"I know, but still, it was quite funny."

"Whatever, anyway why are you out here in daylight and without your minions?"

"I was trying to catch Clive."

Whitton looked down the road at the van as it disappeared into the distance. "Perkins has a first name?" She knew he did, not that she ever intended to use it.

"Don't we all?" He smiled.

They crossed the car park and headed towards the morgue. "Most of us have a personality too. Not Perkins."

"Oh, now Whitton, that is mean. True, but mean." He nudged her with his arm. "What brings you here anyway?" He grabbed the handle to the door and yanked it open, holding it for Whitton to pass through before he followed and let it soft close behind him.

"Not sure, I wanted to go over the reports for Trevor Hayes and Anita Simmons."

"Alright, always happy to oblige you, Sophie." They continued down the corridor that led towards the labs and then on to Barnard's office.

Chapter Twenty-Eight

Whitton perched, as always, on the edge of the antique chair. Barnard poured the tea and she waited patiently. She remembered the first time she had been invited into the sanctuary that was Barnard's office. She had been reprimanded for her brashness and disregard for the finer things in life. She had learnt quickly, never needing a second lesson in anything in life.

With his ritual over, he pushed the delicate china cup and saucer in her direction and took a seat. His eyes roamed her face as he waited for the inevitable questions and summations. He quite liked it that it was always him that she came to when she wanted to talk something through.

"I've been reading up on the reports in all of the Graveyard Killings," she said, her fringe flopping down over her face as she reached forward for the cup. A bony finger slipped into the handle and lifted it to her lips. It was hot; steam still rose from it, and she blew gently. Small ripples ebbed effortlessly. "It's all just... too clean!" she exclaimed, blowing once more before trying a tentative sip.

"Yes, that is something I would agree on. Whoever this chap is, he knows his stuff."

"One of us?" she asked, sliding back into the chair and finally getting comfortable.

"It's always an option. We like to think of ourselves as honest folk. It's always a disappointment to discover we are just as flawed as the natives."

"Hmm. We've got a lead." She watched him perk up, a slight grin upturning the edges of his lips. "Tall, stocky white guy was following Anita."

"Is it Perkins? Please tell me it is and I can finally rid myself of him." The grin grew wider.

"If it is, then I'll buy the first round of drinks. He creeps me out," she admitted.

Barnard tilted his head. "That surprises me. I didn't think anybody could creep you out."

She smiled in return. "Oh, you'd be surprised. I'm only surly and stubborn on the days I don't have my period."

He laughed and poured himself another cup of tea. "How does Rachel tolerate you?"

"She knows what buttons to push." The thought of her lover sent a shot of unexpected arousal straight to her core. She fidgeted. "Anyway, if we can get back to the business of murder? We have a man on video following Anita, and he is wearing blue overalls and a cap."

"Well, that is something. So, what can I do for you?"

"Find me something to link him when I catch him."

He nodded. "I'm waiting on lab results. As you know, we found an oily substance on one of Anita's sleeves. As soon as I know what it is, you'll know. We did find blue fibers on both Anita and Trevor's clothing. Bring me the overalls and I will tell you if they match."

They sat in silence, sipping tea she didn't like. When she had drunk enough that she considered it polite to leave, she placed the cup and saucer gently back down onto the table and pushed it away.

~Grave~

Back at the station, Saint had updated the murder board. Now there were two images, artist impressions that looked similar enough to consider they were the same person. He had dark brows and a scowl that would frighten off most people. His hair was covered with a cap, eyes wearing sunglasses. Whitton thought back to Barnard's joke about Perkins. There was definitely a similarity.

"He looks familiar," Dale said, coming closer to stand beside her. His head tilted one way and then the other.

"Perkins," she stated without emotion. "He looks like Perkins." And someone else, but she couldn't quite put her finger on it.

"Fuck me, he does." Saint laughed. "You don't think?"

"Barnard already checked his roster; he was working when Anita was killed." She turned to him. "Did you find anything else on the video?"

His blonde head shook slowly. "No, nothing."

"Right, grab some copies of those and let's see if we can find anyone that might have seen them."

~Grave~

The street was quiet. It was late afternoon, and most of the residents were either at work or school. Dale Saint parked the car and they both sat staring at the house opposite. The aircon was cool; outside was like a furnace. Diane Boyce was in the garden, knelt down on a foam mat, pulling up weeds.

She looked up from under her hat as the car doors slammed shut. Recognising them, she pulled off her gloves and struggled to her feet, an arthritic knee giving her gip.

"Officers," she acknowledged as they made their way up the path towards her.

"Mrs. Boyce, I wondered if maybe you could take a look at this and tell me if it's anyone you recognise?" Whitton asked as Dale held out the A4 piece of paper with the photofits side by side: two images, the same face, give or take a few discrepancies.

She took it from him and studied it. "I don't think I do. I'm sorry," she said, handing it back to him. "We get a lot of people coming and going, and I am usually quite good at remembering a face. But not his."

Whitton smiled. "No problem. It's always worth asking."

"Is he?" She left the question open, but they all knew what she meant by it.

"We don't know. He is a person of interest, that's all we can really say right now."

Diane nodded. "I still can't believe it, you know. You never think anything like this will happen to anyone you know."

Whitton and Saint said nothing.

"It's the funeral I dread most. Always reminds me of when I lost Frank."

Whitton's lips pursed. "We're sorry for your loss."

"Thank you. It's been a few years now, but you never quite..." She tailed off before shaking her thoughts. "Anyway, if I think of anything else..."

"Please, even if it feels insignificant, just call." Saint smiled and handed her another card with his number on it.

They turned and wandered back down the path, watched all the way by the older woman as she pulled her gloves back on.

"So, where next?" Saint asked, reaching into his pocket for the keys.

"Duncan Simmons, Gina Ashcroft, the pub. Everywhere."

Chapter Twenty-Nine

The team sat around the room at the desks, chairs turned towards Whitton. She had lost O'Leary and Patel to a domestic. A woman had finally had enough and killed the husband, so Whitton was left with Saint, Bowen, and Branson.

"Let's start at the beginning. Dale, I want you to look into Paul Crawford." She tossed a file in his direction. "Andy, take Simmons." Another file landed on the desk. "Jeff, follow up on Hayes." He was closer and held out a hand for the files. She flashed him a grin and picked up the remaining file. "I'll do the dirty work and deal with Herring. I want to know who they knew, who they were talking to or hanging around with, anyone that stood out as suspicious. You know the drill."

The three men stood in unison. "Guv?" Dale said as she watched for Bowen and Branson to exit the room. "I wondered, ya know, if you'd thought any more about...?"

"Yeah, I'd be honoured, Dale."

His face lit up. "Yeah? That's great, Becky will be chuffed. Me too." He laughed nervously. "This little one couldn't ask for a better godmother."

She nodded, biting her lip and holding his gaze. "I will do my best." He nodded back, and she watched him leave before picking up the file and flicking through it. "Time to delve deeper," she mumbled to herself.

George Herring liked little boys, that much was clear. There was a stack of interviews all typed up describing every horrible little detail about Herring, but only Constance Martin had been brave enough to stand up and face him. Unfortunately, the CPS didn't think one person's evidence would be enough, and they were right. Whitton had seen it all too often. Her mind flashed to Rachel, another of life's victims when it came to deviants. Somehow Rachel had made a life for herself and dealt with the demons from her childhood. Her brother had not, and they had seen how that had turned out.

Thinking of Rachel brought a smile to her lips, and she nudged the mouse on her desk, waking the computer. She found the search engine and pulled up options for flower delivery, inputting the details she finished with a final poke of the enter button. A bunch of beautiful flowers would make their way across town to Rachel while Whitton was digging into George Herring's life.

He had met Constance, Martin as she was then, at the local drama club. He was teaching and Constance attended. So had most of the boys, now men, that he had abused. She ran her finger down the list of names of other men the police had spoken to and stopped at one. The name stood out; it was unusual, but it was also a name she had heard before. Galahad Benson.

~Grave~

Mutare was closed this early in the morning, not quite 11 o'clock as Whitton was dropped off by a patrol car. She thanked the PC and waved her off, as there was no need for her to wait around. Whitton would call in when she needed picking up.

She stood outside and looked at the drab building, which had been built in the fifties along with most of Woodington. After the war, towns like this popped up all over, concrete jungles surrounded by row upon row of identical new builds. Now, every space had a block of flats built on it. The high rise was yet to make it to Woodington.

As gardens went, this was one of the scruffiest, but at least the pathway was clear and the bins were tidy. She pushed the gate from its latch and stepped onto the property, already halfway up the path before she heard it clang shut behind her.

The fake smile that greeted her when Jewel Benson opened the door was almost convincing until she remembered Whitton as being a police officer and not a potential new client. She sighed audibly and tilted her head. "I really can't help you with anything more to do with Anita." The sickly smell of incense wafted out and threatened to make Whitton gag.

"Fine, I'm not here to see you. Galahad Benson, he lives here, right?"

The perfectly arched brow rose as Jewel looked down her nose at Whitton. "Of course he lives here."

"Go and get him then, please." She kept her cool, but patience was thinning with this woman. There was no reason for the attitude, and that pricked Whitton's attention. What was she hiding?

"He isn't here," Jewel said quickly, pressing her lips together into a thin smile. "Popped to the shops."

"I see, did you pass him my message to call?"

A slight blush covered the redhead's cheeks and highlighted her freckles. "I...no, sorry, I forgot."

"When will he be back?" Whitton asked, turning slightly at the sound of a car door closing.

"I expect...this afternoon?"

Whitton narrowed her eyes and studied the woman. "You don't seem too sure." The clang of the gate caught her attention and she looked back along the path. DS Saint was walking towards her, eyes narrowed and questioning.

"Guv?" A deep furrow set in between his eyebrows. "What are you doing here?" he asked, looking back and forth between the two women.

"Trying to speak to Mr. Benson," she answered, "What are you doing here?"

"Paul Crawford."

She watched as the woman's eyes widened and her face paled. "What about him?"

Dale turned to Jewel as he spoke. "He was Mrs. Benson's brother."

Chapter Thirty

Whitton and Saint both sat on the sofa now, side by side, watching as Jewel Benson fidgeted with the rings she wore on her left hand. She was an attractive woman, late forties maybe, but life was starting to catch up with her. Her face was freckled but slightly anemic-looking, and up close you could see the pockmarks of an acned youth. Whitton decided, again on closer inspection, that the red hair was most likely a dye job, but a good one, nothing out of a bottle.

"I'm going to be frank, Mrs. Benson, but this is all a little suspicious to me." She looked towards Saint, whose sandy-blonde head nodded sagely. "Constance Martin and Anita Simmons both attended here, and Paul Crawford is your brother. All three are part of my investigation. Now, that's either a very big coincidence, or there is something else going on here."

"There isn't," she said quickly, eyes darting between the pair of them.

Whitton ignored her and sat forward, elbows resting on her knees. "Let's talk about Paul, your brother."

There was a visible tensing of her jaw, and the cords in her neck were rigid. A small bead of sweat dripped from under her fringe to slowly slide towards her cheek. The muscle there twitched as it felt it stroke across the nerve. "What am I supposed to say?" She shrugged and the corners of her mouth turned downwards. "He was my brother, he was trouble, and he got himself killed in a hit and run."

"With his body placed on top of the grave of his own victim," Whitton added to the story.

"How would I know that?" Her indifference was clear.

"You have no knowledge of the circumstances surrounding your brother's death?" Saint interjected.

She glared at him. "I run workshops for those wanting to free themselves from the burden of addiction and life's upheaval. How do you think it would look if I had my brother hanging around, behaving the way that he was?"

"I imagine it would look like you cared about him and were trying to help, even if he didn't want to help himself." Whitton sneered a little at her. "But Paul wasn't an addict, or depressed, was he? He was just trouble, liked to steal cars and drive really fast?"

Jewel cut her eyes at Whitton and looked away. "I couldn't help him."

"You couldn't help him, because he wasn't a drunk, right?" Saint asked. "If he had been, you'd have opened your arms to him, wouldn't you?"

"That's what I do," she bit back.

"People like Anita?" Whitton continued.

"Yes," she said with a hiss. "Anita I could help. Anita and the people she brought with her, they needed to be fixed and we…"

"You and your husband?" Whitton broke in.

Jewel pressed thin lips together and forced a frustrated smile. "Yes, Galahad is a marvel." Her smile was now real and lit up her face as she continued. "He shares his own experiences and allows them to feed off of his energy. It's amazing to watch the transformation."

Whitton caught Saint's brow raise in amusement. "So he shares his experiences with the group?"

Stuttering, she said, "His-his alcohol a-abuse experience, yes." She was fidgeting with her rings again and stopped abruptly when she caught Whitton looking down at her hands.

"And they share their experiences with him?" Dale continued.

Jewel's head moved back and forth between them before eventually she nodded.

"Do you have a photograph of your husband?" Saint asked.

Her mouth gaped open as she considered the question. "I…of course, why do you need one?"

"We have an artist's impression from witnesses."

"You can't possibly think…" She stood up now and placed her palm against her forehead, thinking. "For goodness' sake." She seemed to come to some kind of decision and stomped across the room to the unit. Opening a drawer, she pulled a photo album from it and opened it, holding it out for Whitton to take.

With it in her lap, both Saint and Whitton peered at the picture. A smiling man on his wedding day. A beautiful bride, glowing with happiness. Saint pulled the drawing from his pocket and laid it down flat next to the picture. Galahad Benson was dark-haired, tall and stocky.

They both looked up at Jewel. "We need to speak to your husband," Whitton said as calmly as she could before looking back at the images.

~Grave~

The squad room was buzzing with activity. A new board had appeared, and Galahad Benson's face was central. Black marker pens had scrawled what little information they had on him. Whitton's instructions to dig deep and find out every single thing about him were being taken seriously by Bowen and Branson.

"I'm getting nothing on this guy," Bowen said with his pen in his mouth. "It's like he doesn't exist."

"Name change, it's got to be. If he was born Galahad it would be the easiest record to find. If it's not there, then..." Branson shrugged. "Seriously, who would have called their kid Galahad?" he laughed.

"I heard that Tanner called his kid Tyche, after the Greek God."

Branson's nose wrinkled and the left side of his mouth lifted in a lopsided grin. "Really? Tikey?" he said, looking away from the monitor.

"Ty-kee! Fucking Ty-kee Tanner." They both laughed.

Bowen pinched the bridge of his nose. "Getting back to Sir Galahad, I wonder why he changed his name."

Flicking at a few more keys of his keyboard, Branson grinned. "Because, he was born Derek Galahad Benson." He twisted the monitor so that Bowen could read. "And Derek Galahad Benson is a naughty boy."

Whitton looked up. "I'm going to bring in Jewel Benson."

Chapter Thirty-One

Whitton sat back in her chair and stared at the woman sitting in the seat opposite. They'd been here for less than fifteen minutes. Jewel Benson remained silent.

She felt Saint fidget next to her. He was getting restless already; the room was stifling. Whitton was a patient woman when she needed to be. She could sit here all day if she had to, but Saint was a different prospect. Any minute he was going to blow, and if she was honest, Whitton was looking forward to it. Jewel Benson was probably a little complacent now, content with her silence. She wasn't a woman easily intimidated.

The loud knock on the door interrupted Whitton's thoughts. She stretched her neck and rounded her shoulders before nodding for Saint to open the door. He took the direction and jumped up so fast that his chair screeched back against the floor. Whitton watched as Benson flinched a little before quickly composing herself.

"I don't know what you expect to achieve with this," Jewel said. She was twisted slightly and staring at the "no smoking" sign. "I've done nothing wrong; you can't keep me here forever."

"You can walk right out of here anytime you want," Whitton replied nonchalantly. "As long as you tell me the whereabouts of your husband."

"I don't know, okay?" she finally relented. "He hasn't been home for a few days."

"When did he leave?" Whitton sat forward and picked up her pen, waiting. "All I want to do is talk to him. If he has nothing to do with this then I can rule him out and move on, but right now, Mrs. Benson, right now all I have is a photofit that looks like him and three victims connected to you both. So, the best thing you can do for him is tell me where he is."

She was about to reply when the door opened and Saint returned. "Can I have a word, Guv?"

Outside in the corridor, Saint grinned at her and waved a file in the air. That boyish grin told her they had something.

"Go on, out with it."

"Right, so first of all, we know he was born Derek Galahad Benson in Whitstable, Kent. He grew up there, dropping the name Derek." He grinned again. "When he was 18, he moved to London where he worked as a *plumber*. He got involved in petty thieving, but mostly it was drunk and disorderly stuff until..." He held open the file to her. "He spent five and half years in Scrubs for manslaughter."

"So, he has killed before?"

Saint nodded.

"Okay, let's see if Mrs. Benson knows anything about this."

"One more thing." He touched her arm as she began to turn back into the room. "Jeff found some CCTV from the pub where Trevor Hayes was last seen. There's a bloke on it, looks like a plumber. He evades most of the cameras, but on one he is clearly seen walking into the pub. Then later, he comes back out, with his arm around what looks like a drunk."

"Okay, get Jeff to follow it up."

"He did; landlord doesn't know anything about it. Guv, he's stocky, tall, and wearing a blue boiler suit."

"Alright, let's see if we can find out where the elusive Galahad is hiding."

Jewel Benson looked up at them both as they entered the room again. "What?" she said, noting the knitted brows on both faces.

Whitton took a seat but Saint stood, taking off his jacket and making a show of placing it around the back of his chair. "Mrs....Benson, we have come into some information that I'd like to run past you."

"Is he okay? Did you find him?" she asked urgently. "I don't...it doesn't look good that he isn't here, okay." She seemed to have had a change of heart on remaining silent.

"Doesn't look good?"

"To the clients, if he has…if Galahad has…he did it once before, when we lived in Kent." When Whitton and Saint didn't speak, she continued. Leaning forward, she lowered her voice. "He started drinking again. Took himself off to London and slept on a *friend's* couch."

"And that's where you think he is now?"

She nodded. "If it got out that the very person inspiring others not to drink was a drunk, what do you think would happen to our funding?" Whitton didn't care much for the woman, but she did understand the problem she found herself in. It wasn't Whitton's choice of therapy, but if it worked for some then there was a place for it in Woodington.

"And where does your funding come from?"

"We have a very generous benefactor, actually." She smiled at them both. "Dr. Lydia Robinson and her husband…"

"Jonas?" Whitton asked, her head tilting at the new information.

Jewel Benson looked surprised. "Yes, Jonas helps us when we need legal advice." Whitton noted the information down and waited for Saint to continue with the questioning.

"Mrs. Benson, when you married Galahad, I assume you knew that he had changed his name by deed poll?" he asked.

Her forehead creased, brows knitting tightly together. "What are you talking about?"

Dale smirked. "I am assuming you knew when you married that Galahad had changed his name as well as his lifestyle?"

Slowly, she shook her head. "I don't believe you; he would have told me...he..." Her voice tailed off as Whitton opened the file and slid out a photo of a much younger Galahad Benson facing a police camera and holding a sign with his name clearly written: *Derek G Benson.* "I don't understand."

"Derek Benson is a convicted killer. He was given a ten-year sentence in 1988. He served five and a half years before he was released on probation," Whitton explained as she turned the paperwork around for Jewel to read.

"I don't...that's not the man that I married." Her eyes glistened now as she looked up imploringly at the detectives. "It can't be...there has to be some mistake."

"There is no mistake, Mrs. Benson," Saint assured her. "It's possible that during his time in prison, he straightened himself up, but Galahad Benson and Derek Benson are one and the same."

Jewel pressed her finger against her lip and nibbled at the skin there. "What do you want me to do?"

Chapter Thirty-Two

Whitton had her head in her hands, elbows on the desk as she read through the half inch thick file on Derek Benson. Her stomach grumbled about missing lunch again. Dinner with Rachel tonight couldn't come soon enough. Remembering Dr. Westbrook's words, she picked up her phone and went online. Scrolling through the options, she picked one and paid for it. If she was going to change, then she needed to start somewhere, and today, it seemed, was the day.

"What's got you smiling?" Dale asked, plonking down onto the corner of her desk.

"Just sending Rachel some more flowers," she answered, head back in the file.

"Shit, is it her birthday?" He flustered and jumped to his feet.

Whitton looked up at his concerned face. "No, don't you ever just send flowers to Becky?"

His eyebrow raised. "No, she'd think I was after something."

Whitton chuckled and shook her head. "Maybe you should show her that you're not."

"But I would be." He waggled his brows suggestively.

"Oh, gross." She laughed and tossed a pen at him. "Make yourself useful and fill in the info on the boards. It needs updating."

He left the room and she went back to the file. The more she read, the more interested she became in Derek Benson, AKA Galahad Benson, and his whereabouts now. She made notes of anywhere he might be: places he grew up, went to school, worked. Most of the South East.

"Time to rattle off some emails," she mumbled to herself as she fired up the computer and went through her memory banks for the names of officers who might be able to dig a little and help.

Opening her inbox, the first thing she noticed was an email from Barnard.

```
Subject: re Tox results from oily
Substance/Anita Simmons/Trevor Hayes

Diflucortolone valerate – Found in
Nerisone cream. It's a Corticosteroid
used for reducing inflammation in the
treatment of dermatitis or eczema.

That's all for now.

Tristan
```

She printed it off and added it to the board.

~Grave~

Swigging from her bottle of water, Whitton climbed out of the stuffy car and locked it. There was something different about Rachel's cottage. It was perfectly neat and tidy; the grass was cut and the windows gleamed in the early evening sunlight. Then she spotted it: the for-sale sign.

She downed the last of the water and lifted the recycling bin lid, tossing the plastic bottle in before closing it and opening the gate.

Slipping lose another button on her shirt, she rung the bell before sliding her key into the lock and letting herself in. A brow raised and a smirk appeared on her face as she looked around the familiar place and noted how tidy and clean it was. Rachel had a habit of dropping things as she moved around the house. Her coat invariably ended up on the banister rather than the hook on the wall specifically for it. She would kick her shoes off as she walked through to the lounge rifling through her mail, leaving the envelopes and bills on a side table – the side table that now held a vase filled with fresh flowers.

When Whitton finally laid eyes on her, her breath was taken. She stood with her curvy hips clad in blue jean shorts, her ample cleavage covered in just a bikini top, hair scooped up in a messy ponytail. Sophie's eyes travelled the length of her, taking in the bare feet at the bottom and the gentle lip-biting higher up.

"Before you speak..." Rachel said, walking towards her. When she reached her, she placed a gentle finger against Sophie's lips and smiled. "I have made some decisions these past couple of days, grave decisions, and yes, I probably should have spoken to you about it, but..." She took Sophie's bag from her and placed it down on the sofa. "I should have done this months ago. Whether I move in with you or not, I am selling the cottage." Green eyes stared at Sophie as she waited for a reaction.

"Did you wear this because you wanted to butter me up?" Sophie grinned.

Rachel laughed and twirled. "No, this..." she said, undoing the string at the neck, "...this is for the flowers." She smiled seductively as Sophie's gaze drifted lower, taking in her naked chest. "I thought maybe we could fool around a bit..." The strings behind her back were loosened. "...and then you can take me out to dinner, and then..." She trailed off as she dropped the flimsy material to the floor and reached for the buttons on the shorts. "You can spend however long you want..." Shimmying her hips, she let the bulkier material fall to the ground. "...doing whatever you want with me."

"Anything, huh?" Whitton smirked again, enjoying the sight of Rachel's naked form: every curve, the slight roundness to her tummy, thicker thighs than any of her previous lovers. Rachel turned her on. She glanced up finally and studied her face, with its soft, full lips and those eyes that just saw right through her. Whitton had no doubts, not anymore. "Move in with me."

Rachel's head cocked to one side. She stepped out from the pile of clothing and moved toward Sophie. "Is that what you want?" she asked as the corner of her mouth lifted into the beginnings of a smile that she daren't allow just yet.

Sophie nodded, her dark fringe flopping forward and hiding her eyes. Rachel pushed it away to cup her cheek. She stroked the soft skin there with her thumb and smiled when Sophie's palms gripped her waist and tugged her closer. "And not because I used to see your body at a crime scene, not because I used to panic about not saving you, not for any other reason than I just love you."

Rachel sucked in a breath and held it as she contemplated Sophie's invitation. "I am going to say yes. And not because I can't bear to be in this cottage alone, or because I need you by my side to feel safe, but because I love you and I want to live with you, wake up with you." She kissed the corner of Sophie's mouth. "Cook dinner for you." Another kiss, tugging Sophie's lip between her own. "Mess up your tidy shelves with all the tat I'm going to buy when we go on holidays." She giggled, and this time Whitton took charge, lifting Rachel over her shoulder in a fireman's lift, taking the stairs as speedily as she could before depositing her laughing lover unceremoniously on the bed.

"Absolutely, all of your tat."

Rachel wiggled backwards and lay against the pillows, looking up at Whitton as she pulled her clothes off and tossed them aside without care. When Rachel reached a hand down between her own thighs, she was sure she heard Whitton growl.

Chapter Thirty-Three

Dinner had been nice, a romantic table for two complete with candles and a bottle of wine that Rachel enjoyed more than Sophie. They'd just ordered dessert when Whitton's phone buzzed and vibrated against the table. She sighed and mouthed a rueful 'sorry' across the table to Rachel as she picked up the intrusive device and answered it.

"Whitton." She wasn't on call as such, but the team knew to call her night or day with anything that might even be a sniff of a lead. This was just that. O'Leary was on the other end of the call.

"Sophie, I just took a call from a DI in Kent. Seems he saw the press conference and got in touch."

Whitton straightened in her seat, staring ahead as she took in the information. "Go on."

"There's another one. Another grave killing," she added to clarify. "Happened in a place called Molesden, tiny little village outside of Canterbury."

"Okay, I'm on my way in." She was already standing, dropping the napkin that had lain across her lap onto the table. She looked at Rachel. A thin-lipped smile said it was fine, but she hated doing it.

"Fine, I've got the details. But Guv? It's not new."

"What do you mean?"

"This one happened 17 years ago."

Whitton sat back down and picked up her glass. She swirled the liquid in the glass before putting it back down on the table and leaning forward, her elbow on the table as she ran her fingers through her hair.

"Alright, can you email me what you have? I'll read it tonight, and then tomorrow me and you will be heading to Kent."

O'Leary seemed to perk up at that news. "Road trip? Great, I'll bring a packed lunch."

"Okay. Don't forget to email."

"I am doing it now."

Whitton hung up and placed the phone down onto the table. It instantly beeped a notification of mail.

"If you have to go, it's okay," Rachel said just as the waitress reappeared with dessert. She looked down at the cheesecake Sophie had ordered. "I can get that take-away."

Whitton looked down at the cheesecake too. It looked delicious. Shaking her head, she picked up the spoon and heard Dr. Westbrook's words in her head. *You have to decide if she is worth it to you, and if she is, then you are the one that has to put her first.* "No, it can wait. I'm spending the evening with you."

Rachel's smile told her all she needed to know. It was the right decision.

~Grave~

Dale Saint met Whitton in the car park when she arrived the following morning. He didn't look happy as she dropped her cigarette butt and ground it out. He stalked across to her as she bent down and picked it up. "Why is O'Leary going with you today and not me?"

She stood up and looked at him. His face flushed a little when he realised how churlish he sounded.

"No reason. She called with the information and I said she could come with me. I was hoping you'd step up while I was gone and deal with things from this end but, if you'd rather that I leave Colleen in charge and you come for a drive..."

"No, that's..." He ran a hand through his short, fair hair. "You're leaving me in charge?"

"That's the plan. I figured you could organise the troops and chase up the CCTV around the church with Jeff." She started to walk towards the office as she shoved her cigarette litter bag back into her pocket.

"Are you ever going to chuck that?" Dale said, jutting his chin towards the pocket containing the bag.

"Probably," she replied. "So, you alright now? Hissy fit over?"

He caught up with her. "It wasn't a hissy fit," he refuted, but with no real enthusiasm.

"Yes, it was. But I won't tell anyone." She leaned towards him and whispered as two uniforms passed. "Oh, by the way, are you free at the weekend?"

"Might be, depends what the offer is and whether I get to go on the next jolly-up."

Whitton laughed. "A day out with me isn't ever going to be a jolly-up, is it?"

"Fair point. What do you want me to do?"

She stopped them as they reached the door, letting two officers out as she held the door open. "Rachel's moving out of the cottage."

"Bout fucking time. Gives me the creeps knowing she's still in there," he said without thinking. "Sorry."

"It's fine, gives me the creeps too. Anyway, she's moving…in with me."

He laughed, his head flung back. "I knew it wouldn't be long. All that shit about not rushing it after Yvonne." He grinned at her. "I'm happy for ya, Soph. Yvonne was alright, but Rachel…she gets you. I'll be over about 10, that okay?"

"Yeah, thanks, Dale."

~Grave~

Molesden was a picturesque village in rural Kent. It had the quintessential cricket green and thatched-roof pub. St. Saviour's Church had been built in the 17th century and was tiny in comparison to its 11th century neighbour, Canterbury Cathedral, just 12 miles away to the east. Colleen O'Leary pulled her car into the small side road and parked.

"Hard to believe anything sinister could happen somewhere like here, eh?" she said, looking out of the windscreen as she switched the engine off. The scene looked like a puzzle box picture.

"According to TV, these kinds of places are a hotbed of evil, wrongdoing, and murder," Whitton said pushing the file she had been reading back into her satchel. When she glanced across at Colleen and found her staring blankly, she added. *"Midsummer? Touch of Frost?"* When Colleen shook her head, she rolled her eyes. "Seriously? *Vera?"*

"I don't really watch TV. Mike prefers a movie, so we have those cinema cards where you can go as many times as you want."

"Right. Well, anyway. Shall we go in and meet DI Wilcox?"

Standing in the graveyard beside the well-kept tomb they'd all come to see was a tall man. His hair was greying, matching the colour of his well-worn suit. He waved a hand in their direction and both women walked towards him.

"DI Whitton." He held out a hand and she shook it.

"Yeah, this is O'Leary. Thanks for meeting with us."

"How could I not? This case has bothered me for years, and now there's a chance we might solve it," he said seriously.

"That's the plan. So, what can you tell us?"

"Well..." He turned around and pointed down at a headstone. It was made of black marble and looked quite new in terms of many of the others.

Kevin Maxim

12th May 1967 – 4th Aug 1992

Rest in Peace

"Kevin Maxim was the local simpleton, for want of a better word. He was the kid that did any dare. Like a sheep, he followed the gang, and it was always him that got caught for anything."

Whitton listened as O'Leary took notes.

"He broke into a house in the village, for a dare. Came face to face with the owner, Brian

Pickford, and panicked, pushed him out of the way and unfortunately Brian toppled down the stairs."

"So, you arrested him? How did you know it was him?" Whitton asked.

"He owned up. Like I said, simpleton. Not a bad lad, just led astray. We charged him with manslaughter."

"But he got off?" O'Leary piped up while still scribbling the information.

"His brief argued that he wasn't of sound mind, and to be fair..." He shrugged his shoulders, lips set in a firm thin smile. "Who were we to argue? We all knew he was an idiot."

He started walking, and Whitton and O'Leary followed around the side of the building to a shadier part of the cemetery. Here was another headstone, this time a granite one, beautifully chiseled with an angel on the top corner and the words:

Brian Pickford

23rd Dec 1937 – 9th June 1992

Always remembered.

Always loved.

"This is where we found Kevin. Laid out neatly. His neck broken."

"Gotta say, it matches ours to a tee. Did you have any suspects?" Whitton asked.

Wilcox smiled sadly. "Nope, I was the lead on the case back then. New to the job and that but, I'd grown up around here; I knew Kevin. He wasn't a bad lad. If anything, his mates should have been the ones charged, but we all know the law, right?"

Both women nodded.

"Thing is, we had no idea what it was about. Assumed it was some kind of retribution from someone Brian knew, but with no real evidence and nothing much else to go on, it slipped into the cold case pile."

Whitton's interest was piqued. "No real evidence? You mean you did have something?"

Wilcox chuckled. "Kevin had someone else's DNA under his index fingernail."

Chapter Thirty-Four

The drive back from Kent felt like the longest journey of Whitton's life. She floored the accelerator and exceeded the speed limit by just enough that she wouldn't get a ticket. O'Leary held on with one hand and tried again to get hold of Saint.

"Nope, no signal out here. I'll try again when we hit the motorway."

Whitton checked the time on the dashboard. It was 2.15 p.m. "Don't worry about it. We should be back in an hour if the traffic plays fair."

"True, and it's not like we can do anything with it. Kent needs to send it through to Barnard, and then we still need someone to match it to."

A blue Volvo sped past and Whitton honked her horn at it. "Bloody idiot. It's not like I'm driving slowly," she complained. The country lanes were bendy and barely wide enough for two cars to pass each other, but she was confident enough to navigate them safely. She'd been on enough driving courses, after all. "If we find him in a ditch up ahead, I'm not stopping."

O'Leary chuckled and put the seat back. "Wake me up when we get back."

Whitton eased off the accelerator a little, keeping one eye on the sat nav for the turning that would lead them down onto the M20. Colleen was already snoring lightly when it came, and Whitton took the turning slowly so as not to wake her.

While the car did all of the hard work, Whitton let her mind wander over the case. She thought about each set of victims. How would anyone come into contact with them all? She guessed that there were newspaper reports, and in the case of Kevin Maxim, a small village where everyone knew everything. The more she thought about it, the more she leaned towards someone in the medical field, or someone closely attached to the emergency services. They had to have inside information somehow. She thought about Rachel; maybe the suspect was married to a nurse? A paramedic? A copper even, maybe they were a copper? She shook her head. Hayes' murder was too precise; it had to be someone with medical knowledge.

She sighed as red lights on the cars up ahead all began to light up together. Traffic; just what she didn't need.

~Grave~

The four-car pile-up on the M20 had delayed them by almost two hours. Whitton's phone battery had died, and O'Leary was annoyed that her phone still wouldn't pick up a signal.

"I'm going to bloody well take this back. It's only a month old. It's supposed to be the latest thing out there," she complained as Whitton pulled into the yard. She had a headache brewing, and Colleen's constant chatting since waking 20 minutes into the traffic jam was starting to grate. "And you don't have a charger? I'm going to get you one. Everyone needs a charger," she continued on, and Whitton cricked her neck one way and then other before she pulled into her spot and yanked the handbrake.

She climbed out of the car and stalked off, leaving Colleen to call after her that the car wasn't locked. The loud beep made Colleen jump as Whitton held the fob over her shoulder and pressed the lock button.

When she reached the office, she found Branson with his feet up on the desk and Bowen perched on the corner. They were laughing over a cup of coffee.

"Comfortable?" she asked, staring down at them as Branson pulled his feet from the desk and sat up.

"Guv."

"I'm out of the office for one day and you all think it's a day off?"

Colleen bustled into the room and dumped her bag on her desk. Her phone suddenly sprang into life and notifications beeped as several came through now the phone seemed to have service. Whitton ignored it. Her glare held on the two men in front of her. "Where's Saint?"

"Interview room," Bowen said quickly. "Galahad Benson, he's interviewing him."

Her brow rose and arched. "How did that happen?"

"The wife called about an hour ago, said he had turned up and you wanted to know about it. Dale and Ansu went and got him. They're both interviewing him now."

"Great, go down there and get a DNA swab," she ordered. "Get it sent to Barnard ASAP."

Branson stood, his eyes narrowing at her. "Guv?"

"He wasn't always this clever." She grinned.

~Grave~

Galahad Benson was a tired man. He slumped in the chair they made him sit in and tried to focus. The past few weeks had exhausted him, but finally he had his head together.

Now though, as he sat across from the two coppers, he wondered if he had made a big mistake. He was just grateful that Jonas Robinson was sitting beside him.

They'd been pummeling him for over an hour. Where had he been? Could anyone vouch for that? He'd literally just walked through the door when Jewel had launched at him, screaming about murder and god-only-knows what. And then there was banging on the door and before he knew it, he was being handcuffed and led away. It brought back memories of a time he had tried to forget. Maybe it was useless, maybe he would never forget; that was probably the truth of it. He couldn't outrun his past. He couldn't change who he was. The man he had become was because of the past, but it still haunted him.

When the door opened and a black guy poked his head around it, Galahad took the opportunity to close his eyes and enjoy the reprieve from the constant inane questions.

Last week had been a blur. All he remembered was turning up at the pub. Such a brave thing to do, daring in fact. In his own back yard and where anyone could have seen him. Now look where that had got him.

The one in charge waffled something about the interruption, for the tape. Then he stood up. The legs of the chair scraping against the floor hurt Galahads teeth, and sucked in his cheeks. All he needed to do was just sit still and stay quiet.

When Saint returned, he had a box in his hand that he put to one side before continuing on with the interview, Ansu doing the usual reminders for the tape.

"Tell me about Anita Simmons," Saint asked casually.

"She used to come along to Mutare," he acknowledged. "After one of her clients introduced her."

"Which client?"

"I don't know." He rubbed his face and scratched at his stubbled chin. "Tall woman, Connie or something."

"Constance Martin?"

"Yeah, that might be it. Look, what does this have to do with me?"

"We will get to that, Mr. Benson. I just want to clarify that you knew Anita Simmons, Constance Martin, and Paul Crawford?"

His face scrunched up in confusion. "Paul? What does Paul have to do with anything? He's dead."

Sharp knuckles rapped against the door, and Saint stood to answer it.

"For the tape, 16.34, DS Saint has left the room," Patel said aloud. They sat in silence and waited.

Saint returned a couple of minutes later. Closing the door behind him, he grinned as he stared across the room at a disheveled Benson and his solicitor, Jonas Robinson.

"You've lived in Kent too, haven't you?" he said, crossing the room and taking his seat. "See the thing is, Mr. Benson, we have cause to believe that you might be responsible for a little vigilantism, not just here in Woodington, but in Kent as well."

He waited for Benson's reaction and got none. Robinson stayed quiet too, but he was much more alert now, sitting up in his chair and adjusting his collar.

"What exactly are you accusing my client of?"

"Murder, Mr. Robinson."

Benson surged forward and roared, "What? You're not fitting me up again!" Robinson reached an arm across his chest and eased him back in his seat. "This is a fit up."

Ignoring his client's protests, Robinson asked, "I assume that you have evidence to back this ridiculous claim up?"

Saint pulled a photo from the file. Placing it on the desk, he turned it with his fingers and slid it towards Benson. "This man is someone we believe is connected to the murder of at least three people here in Woodington." He looked across to Robinson. "As you can see, there is a very good likeness to Mr. Benson."

"He looks a lot like me too," Robinson laughed. "This isn't proof that the man in the photo is indeed my client." He smirked now. "And secondly, even if it were, you have nothing to link him to an actual crime. Unless looking like somebody is a crime these days?"

Now it was Saint's turn to smirk. "Actually, we might."

Chapter Thirty-Five

Galahad Benson fidgeted in his seat. "I'm not giving you my DNA." He shook his head at the swab that Saint had pulled from the almost-forgotten box.

"Then tell us where you have been all this time. The sooner you give us something we can corroborate, the sooner you are out of our line of inquiry," Ansu Patel said, his dark eyes boring into Benson. "It's a bit of a coincidence that you are missing at the same time not one, but two people are murdered in Woodington, isn't it?"

Benson continued to stare back at him. Finally, he leant in to his brief and spoke quietly. Robinson nodded.

"My client is happy to make a statement on one condition." Saint stared impassively until he continued. "My client would prefer that whatever he tells you now remains between us and that his wife doesn't find out."

"We will do our best; however, should Mr. Benson be charged with anything, then I cannot guarantee that the CPS and future prosecution representatives won't use it against him."

Robinson smiled confidently and then nodded at his client.

Benson cleared his throat. "I was in London. Visiting a friend." His face flushed and he looked away.

"And this friend's name would be?" Pen poised, Saint peered up at him.

Benson glanced across at his brief once more. Receiving the affirming nod, he continued. "Sally, Sally Taylor." He sighed and rubbed his face.

"I see, and Ms. Taylor can confirm that you were there for the entire time that you have been missing."

He nodded and licked his lip. "Yeah. Look, I...Jewel, you know she's the love of my life, but sometimes..." He shrugged. "I lose my way from the path."

"You don't need to explain that to us. I'll need a number and details of the address so that I can confirm," Saint said as both he and Patel prepared to finish the interview. "Oh, and Mr. Benson, I still need that DNA sample."

~Grave~

Flopping into the chair opposite her, Dale Saint exhaled loudly. "It ain't him."

Whitton stopped what she was doing and leaned back in her chair to listen. "Why not?"

"He's an old drunk getting his end away. Twenty quid says that DNA comes back negative."

"Then we're back to square one again."

Saint grinned. "Are you sure it ain't Perkins?"

Whitton laughed and picked up her pen again. "If only." She started writing again. "Barnard said he was working when Anita was killed, so unless he's working with a twin?"

"Bugger. Right, well I am going home. Unless you want me to do anything else?"

She checked her own watch; it was nearing seven, "Nope, get lost. I'm just typing this up and then I'll be following." She watched him leave, waving over his shoulder. Colleen had gone a while ago. Jeff was taking the DNA sample over to Barnard, and Bowen hadn't been in today; dentist's appointment. Patel was still typing at his desk, so the office wasn't empty, but it felt quiet, which was why it felt loud when her email beeped a new message.

Sender: JUdGeAnDExecuTioNer@Hotmail.com

Subject: You're wasting your time.

DI Whitton. If you lot did your job better, then I would not need to clean up after you. These are grave times and the unpunished must be taken to task. You'll never find me. Nobody else has.

I am the law.

"Oh, That's just great. Now you're taunting me," she mumbled to herself as she picked up the phone to call IT.

"Nobody else has ever found me? Well, let the challenge begin."

~Grave~

Whitton walked into the internet café on Grafton Street and looked around. Clearly the place had once been a retail shop, some of the shelving still up along the wall on the left with computers and secondhand games for sale. Neon signs flashed in the window, and the low hum of dance music could be heard coming from a stereo somewhere. Small desks lined the centre of the room, back to back and pushed up close against one another with a wooden wall between each one for privacy.

Most were empty. The odd head could be seen, bowed down as someone typed or played a game, but nobody looked up. She walked the entire length of the shop, noting one camera in the back and one up front.

"Bingo," she mumbled to herself as she strolled over to the guy with headphones on behind the till. He had his eyes closed as his head bobbed rhythmically to the music he was listening to. Using her index finger, she tapped him twice on the forehead, making him jump.

"What the fuck?" He looked annoyed as he put the headphones around his neck, not that she cared. The tinny noise of the band he was listening to floated into the air.

Holding up her warrant card, she smiled sarcastically at him. "DI Whitton, I'd like to see your CCTV for the last two hours."

He fiddled with his iPod and switched off the music. "You'll be lucky...it hasn't worked for months. The owner is supposed to get it fixed but like, why bother. Look at it in here." His eyes cased the area just like hers had done when she first arrived. "Nobody comes in here for trouble, they're all too busy with the latest game or checking out the sites they can't at home." He chuckled; she didn't.

"About an hour ago, did you notice a tall, well-built man come in?"

He shrugged. "Get a lot of them."

"This one would be older, fifties maybe."

His mouth lifted on one side as he thought about it. "There was this one guy, looked like a plumber."

"Blue overalls?"

"Yeah, bit odd I suppose, we don't tend to get workmen in here that often."

"Did you see his face?"

He scrunched up his cheek again. "Not really, I don't pay much attention you know. They hand over their money and I free up a screen. He had sunglasses on and a cap, wasn't much to see." He seemed to consider things for a moment. "His hair was grey, here." He fingered his own hair around his ear.

She felt the rush of excitement start to flood her nervous system. "Which booth did he use?" Her eyes swept the area once more as he pointed to one right at the front of the store. "Has anyone else used it since?"

"No. Look, what is this about?"

"I'm going to need you to close up," she said, grabbing her phone and calling the crime scene techs.

Chapter Thirty-Six

The following morning, Whitton all but frog-marched Saint down to the internet café. It was closed now, the street quiet. There was a welcome chill in the air as the sun was yet to warm up.

"So, I was thinking," Dale said as he tried to keep up.

"Don't do that, Dale, you might damage something." She smirked at him over her shoulder and slowed her pace.

"Funny," he snarked back. "But seriously, why send you an email, why taunt you? He hasn't ever done that before, has he?"

"Not that we know of." She stopped marching and looked up and around. "Did you tell Jeff to wait around?"

"Yep, he is all set and already onto the council for access to the street cams."

"Good. My gut says we won't get much from them. Look how the overhang covers anyone walking beneath it." The buildings had been built in the 50s, shop fronts with flats and offices above. The entire length of the building had a flat-roofed overhang that allowed shoppers to peruse windows without the weather bothering them.

Saint exhaled. "So why are we here?"

She spun around and smiled at him. "Because..." Her head moved and twisted to the left, towards a phone repair store that sold used handsets, phone covers, and chargers. "See that flashing red light back there?" They both peered into the shop opposite at the CCTV camera trained on the front window and door. "The owner is coming in early to open up and give us the tape."

"Sometimes, I just wanna kiss you." Dale grinned. "Instead, I'll go get us coffee while we wait."

She waited by the window, a lonely figure in a desolate street. The strains of Beethoven began ringing out loudly from her pocket.

"Hello." She smiled into the handset.

"Morning, I missed you. I woke up and you were gone already," Rachel whined casually.

"Yeah, had an early start. I didn't want to wake you though, you looked..." She checked over her shoulder for Dale. Seeing the coast was clear, she continued. "If I woke you up, I might not have gone to work," she finally admitted with a chuckle.

"Ah, I see, that's a shame then. Because that's my favourite way to wake up," Rachel purred, and Whitton felt herself shiver with arousal. "I'm going to have to take care of this...need, all by myself, Detective." She spoke slowly and confidently, knowing full well the effect she was having on her detective.

"I tell you what, you hold off for now and I will make it worth your while tonight."

"Promises, promises, Sophie. Don't keep me waiting too long. I'm not sure I'll be able to hold off if you're late."

Whitton grinned. "I love you, see you later."

"Likewise, Detective."

She put the phone back into her pocket just as Dale returned to hand her a coffee. "Everything all right? You look a bit...flushed."

"Yeah, all good," she replied, sipping the hot liquid. Their attention was grabbed then by a middle-aged man in a turban walking towards them.

"DI Whitton? We talked on the phone," he said, pulling a set of keys from his jeans pocket. He found the key he needed and opened the door. A loud beeping started as the alarm kicked in. Whitton and Saint followed him in and waited as he disarmed it. "Bloody noise." He grinned and turned back to the door. "Do us a favour and lock that. Otherwise I'll have punters in here before I open."

Saint flicked the catch and locked the door.

"So, you need the tape for the last 24 hours?" he continued, far too chatty and chipper for this early in the morning as far as Whitton was concerned, but she nodded and replied.

"Yes, if that's possible."

"Sure, you wanna look at it first?"

Nodding, Whitton moved forward. "That would be great."

~Grave~

The tiny office out back doubled up as a workshop, canteen, and staff room. There was a small table with a screen on it, surrounded by phone parts and tools. A dirty, empty mug was growing something green inside it, and Mr. Chatterjee moved it quickly out of the way as Saint took the seat in front of the screen.

"Sorry 'bout that, I get busy and forget, ya know."

"No problem. If you can get the tape then..." Whitton smiled a thin-lipped smile.

He fiddled with a small machine and held up the SD card. "Bit better than a tape," he said, slotting it into the space it fit. "So, it's a pretty simple system. Just hit rewind or fast forward. Then play and stop," he said, showing them how it worked.

"Thanks," Saint replied. "We shouldn't be too long." He waited for Chatterjee to get the message that they didn't need him hanging around.

With the owner out of the room, Saint hit play and started forwarding the recording. "What time did the email arrive?"

"Just after seven. So I imagine he arrived a few minutes before and left pretty much right after he sent it." The world outside sped past the window, occasional browsers stopping to look at something. Now and then the door would open and someone would walk in and speak to the owner. Just an average day in Woodington.

When the timer reached 18:50, Dale stopped the fast forward and let it play. It was still light out. People were still milling around, walking past on their way home from a day of working or shopping, or heading into town for a few drinks, or a dinner. At 18:58, Whitton's heart raced as a man in blue overalls stepped into shot. There was something about his gait, the way he held himself, that felt familiar to her, but trying to recognise him behind the disguise was impossible.

There was nothing else to see until 19:06 on the timer. As he came out, he couldn't avoid the camera right in front of him. He clearly didn't know it was there, as he made no attempt to hide his face. Saint hit pause, and a slightly out of focus image appeared. "Something about him looks familiar," he said, "I feel like I have spoken to him."

"Yeah, I feel like that too." She leaned in over Saint's shoulder and placed her palm on the screen, covering the eyes and top of his head. "Something about his mouth...play it again."

Dale did as he was asked and rewound the segment, letting it play at normal speed. "There's nothing."

"Back it up, play it again." They watched the screen intently. "What's that? What does he do there?" She pointed at the screen as the man's hand disappeared from sight.

"Putting something in his pocket or...pulling something out." He stood up and left the room. Whitton followed as he ran up to the door, unlocked it and moved with speed out into the street and over towards the internet café. Head bowed, his eyes scoured the floor and then he bent down, reaching into his pocket for a glove.

"What is it?" Whitton said from behind him.

When he turned back, he was grinning. "It's a matchbook, from The Blue Room."

The Blue Room was Woodington's one and only gentleman's club, a term that most people knew actually meant strip joint.

"Yes! Right." She pushed her hand through her hair and sucked in a calming breath. "Let's get this all to forensics."

Chapter Thirty-Seven

A partial print and the name of a strip club, that was what they had to go on. It was at least a lot more than they previously had, and for some reason most of the blokes were pretty eager to do the legwork. One by one they sauntered into Whitton's office and made the case for why they should be the one who visited the Blue Room later that night. It was comical really, and Whitton let them egg each other on about who would get the nod. The banter and laughter were welcomed in the office, which was usually filled with the depths of death and despair at not being able to catch a killer.

Eventually, she needed to put them all out of their misery. Checking her watch, she saw it was just coming up to five in the afternoon. She had a long day ahead of her tomorrow with Rachel moving in, so she didn't want a late night tonight.

"Right, listen up," she called out into the main office. Voices quieted, except for Bowen, who was on the phone talking in a hushed tone. "Okay, Colleen, you're finished on that domestic, right?"

"Yep, all wrapped up and passed onto the CPS." Colleen smiled at her boss.

"Great, I want you to come with me now down to the Blue Room." The room erupted into groans and complaints as O'Leary laughed at them all. "And then," she said, waiting for quiet again. "Jeff and Andy, I want you to go down later tonight and…" She grinned at them. "Enjoy the show." Whoops and laughter, along with a few comments that Whitton instantly frowned at, burst forth. "Okay, okay, calm it down, this is work. I want eyes in the room. Make a note of anyone that fits our criteria."

"Alright, boss." Jeff acknowledged the seriousness of it.

"Right."

"Uh, what about me?" Saint piped up as he swiveled his chair around.

"Oh, I'll have plenty for you to do when I get back."

~Grave~

The Blue Room wasn't blue in colour. It had clearly got its name from the connotations of porn and naked girls. Inside it was all reds and pinks, glitter and sparkly. The walls and chairs were covered in the same material, all soft and plush. O'Leary flashed her badge at the insolent women who opened the door to them, pointing without speaking towards the bar when they asked for the manager.

"It's like being inside a giant vagina," O'Leary whispered.

Whitton turned slowly. "And you'd know all about that, I suppose."

O'Leary's face reddened, but she grinned. "You'd be surprised what I know." She winked, and Whitton grinned at the shared communication.

"I see, well if the one you've met was this glittery, I'd get her to a doctor." She winked back.

Even in the daylight, it was still dark inside. The lights were on, cleaners and bar staff moving around with no real interest as they got the place ready for another night entertaining a mainly male audience. In front of them as they walked between the tables and podiums stood a blonde man, no more than five and a half feet in stature with a robust frame. His suit had clearly needed to be made to measure.

"Anders Jacob?" Whitton asked, the J sounding like a Y. His smile was warm and friendly as he turned to see who it was that called his name.

"Ja, that's me," he replied, a slight accent to his voice.

"DI Whitton, this is DC O'Leary. I wondered if we could have a word?" she asked, looking around at all the prying eyes as workers came to a halt. Police in the building usually wasn't a good sign.

He tilted his head and pointed to a table.

"In private, if you don't mind?"

He looked the dark-haired officer up and down through narrowing eyes before seeming to come to a conclusion. "Of course, please follow me."

He led them through the bar and out into a hallway that led to some stairs. The décor here wasn't quite as plush as the other side of the bar. Boxes of crisps stacked up against the wall alongside crates of bottled drinks and a hoover. The office was a boxy little room with a desk and some filing cabinets.

"So, what can I help you with?" he said as he rounded the desk and sat down gently into the chair. his frame filling the seat and bulging through the sides.

Whitton pulled a photo of the matchbook from her pocket and held it out to him. "These are yours, right?"

Studying the photo briefly, he nodded. "Yes, they are. It clearly says the Blue Room on there."

"Tell me about them?"

His eyes narrowed again at her and he opened the drawer to his left, reached in, and rifled through before he pulled out an exact copy, tossing it on the desk. "We give them out to anyone who wants one."

"And they all have this design?" she asked, picking up the one he had thrown.

"Yes. Well, no, actually we just had a new batch printed, a few minor changes on it, but you wouldn't notice. That one had a mistake. They used the wrong font."

"So how many of these were handed out?"

He shrugged and laughed. "Not a clue, we ordered 1000, most are in a box for the bin."

"I'd like a copy of your membership list," Whitton said without preamble.

He laughed. "No, not a chance."

Sighing audibly, she glared at him. "Don't make me get a warrant, or worse, find a reason to come down here and start poking around."

"Look, what do you want to know?"

"I want the names of anyone who could potentially have been given one of these."

He thought for a moment before he too sighed and reached for the drawer again. "I can make this a whole lot easier, but on one condition: the information didn't come from me. I can't have people thinking their privacy is at odds with our policy." He held his hands out, palms up. When he received a nod from Whitton, he continued. "Those were handed out on the day they arrived, and again the following night. The minute the problem was pointed out, we stopped giving them away."

"Right, and this helps me how?"

He grinned at her. "Patience. Every member has a membership card, it's a chip and pin, bit like your bank card, only these register the date and time that they entered and left, what they bought. It helps us work out who our more financially viable customers are, if you see what I mean?"

Whitton felt the goosebumps hit her spine. "So you can tell me every punter that potentially had one of these?"

He nodded. "Of course, that's if they took one. And..." He paused. "If they kept it and didn't give it away."

"How quickly can you get me that list?"

"I just need to print it off."

Chapter Thirty-Eight

"Anyone who is white, older than 40, darker haired." Whitton gave the instructions to the team. She split the list of names between them all, so each had 25 or so names to go through the databases with and start to whittle it down to potential men they could talk to. "You all know what we are looking for. if they fit the descriptions, then pull their file and print a photo. I want them all on my desk within the hour. Let's get this creep."

The sound of keys being tapped and paper being rifled through was music to Whitton's ears as she sat down with her own list of names. The Blue Room was a pretty busy place most nights of the week by the look of it, but especially busy over the weekend when these matchbooks had been available. She ran a finger down the list and noted a couple of names she knew. A couple of local politicians, a high-ranking officer, and the head teacher of the local Catholic school. She blew out a breath and tapped in the first name; she didn't care about their morals, unless they were slaughtering people in their spare time.

Ryan Cappley. She typed his name in and a face appeared on screen. Blonde, early twenties. She clicked to move on. Artur Grokalski, Bald. too young. From her list, just 8 made the cut and fit the bill; one was the head teacher, Patrick Shaughnessy.

She glanced up and noticed her colleagues still hard at it. The tiny ping of an email coming in caught her attention and reminded her that she hadn't checked it for days. When she clicked it open, she didn't expect to find an entire page of unopened mail.

There were the usual updates and newsletters she always got. Tristan's recordings sent through so she had an e-copy as well as the hard-copy he would send by courier. What she wasn't used to seeing were emails from addresses she didn't know: fellow officers at different forces. She opened the first and scanned quickly through the detail, printed it off, and quickly opened the next, doing the same, then the next and so on until she had 12 pieces of paper from officers around the country all reporting a grave murder in their area. The earliest was February 1993, and they continued right through till just a year before George Herring had been murdered in Woodington.

"Dale," she called out through the open door. When she had his attention, she waved him over. "Get in here."

He wandered over like a schoolboy about to get a detention. "I am going as fast as I can…"

"Oh shut up. Close the door and sit down," she demanded. He looked relieved that he wasn't getting a bollocking. "I just went through my email."

"That's what you called me in here for…all secret squirrel." He grinned, and she glared.

"Yes. Do you want to listen, or…?"

"Sorry, yes. I'm just knackered. Harry is being a little…" He sighed. "Anyway, what did you discover?"

She handed over the pile of freshly printed paperwork and sat silently while he read the first, then the second, and then frantically flicked through the rest. His face was ashen. "Holy fuck," he finally said, looking up at her. "What the hell have we got here?"

"Something bigger than we all assumed. And whoever it is, is now here." She leant forwards and put her arms on the desk. "How many names you got left on your list?"

"Nine or ten, I dunno." He yawned. "Sorry, it just...Harry was up all night again. She isn't too impressed with the idea of a new baby."

"Dale, fucking focus," she hissed. "I love your kids, but time and fucking place, alright?" Her left hand dragged through her hair. "Look, give Jeff the rest of your list. Then I want you to get all of the names put aside so far and start going through them. Find out where they're from, where they work, places they've lived." Sitting back in her chair, she added, "This is it. I can feel it. Someone is going to stand out."

"Alright, I can do that. What about you?"

"I need to speak to the Chief."

~Grave~

It took hours, but as each detective finished up their original list, they started on the next. Anything that linked any man to any place where a murder had taken place was noted down. Whitton ordered in pizza. Six large boxes lay open on the desk, the insides now demolished as hungry bellies were fed.

"Fuck me," Dale said to himself loudly enough that everyone stopped what they were doing. "I think I've got him, Soph." He turned to face her, his face as serious as she had ever seen it. Standing, she moved across the room and leant in over his shoulder to look at the screen.

"Jesus," she agreed. Straightening up, she blew out a breath. "Run it by me," she said, her eyes glued to the murder board, to Anita's face.

"Jonas David William Robinson." He said the name clearly and concisely.

"Fuck off, the defence solicitor from the court?" Andy Bowen asked, his own voice incredulous as Saint nodded.

Whitton's head swiveled towards the interruption, and Saint continued on. "Age 57. Married to Dr. Lydia Jane Thomson. He was born in Harrogate. Lived there until he was twelve, when his mother died and he ended up moving in with an aunt. His dad was on the scene but in the navy, so away a lot."

"Where did the aunt live?" Whitton asked, her eyes back on the photo of Anita.

"York. That's where he stayed until Uni. He went to Durham. Got his law degree and then…"

Whitton turned back to face him. "The mother, what did she die from?"

Saint opened another tab and tapped away on the keys, reading from the screen as the information appeared. "Natural causes. Nothing suspicious about it."

She pinched her lower lip between her fingers while she thought about it. "Something set him off, something that wasn't fair. Something where someone got away with it."

Dale nodded. "Yeah, but what? It says here, he got his law degree and then first job straight out of Uni. We don't get our first Grave Murder until 1993. By that time, he is what? Thirty years old?"

"Ansu? You and Colleen, start going over his cases. See if there is anything that stands out."

"Guv, one problem with that." It was Jeff who now offered his opinion. "He never murders anyone from his own cases."

"That's true, but the likelihood is, whatever set him off is personal. And if it's not a family member or someone linked to him, then maybe it's a case that went wrong. Just look will you, cross those T's, alright? I want this fucking airtight by the time we take this to the CPS." She raised a brow. "They won't want to touch it unless it's an absolute. And once we tip our hand, he knows we know."

"He has worked or lived in or around every murder site," Dale added. "And the first one here happened one month after him and his wife moved in."

"She's a vet," Whitton said under her breath and then much louder. "The wife, she's a vet. When I ran into him at the court, he said she ran a practice from home. Hayes was injected with ketamine. So were most of these victims." She held up the pile of papers. "Let's get all of our ducks in order, timelines, everything, and then I want warrants for a search. I want tyre prints ASAP."

"It's going to take some time, Guv."

She knew that it would. In her old life she would work them all through the weekend until every I had been dotted, every T crossed, and they'd chased down the culprit. But that wouldn't work this time. An image of Rachel flashed into her mind and she remembered that in the morning, she was moving in, something Whitton was looking forward to. "I know. Look, get what you can done today. Then Monday we go at it, all hands on deck. Alright?"

Chapter Thirty-Nine

Saturday morning found Whitton awake too early. She picked up the hire vehicle and drove it over to Dale's. As soon as he opened his mouth to moan about the time, she thrust a coffee into his hand and smiled.

"I know it's early. I just want to get this done without scaring her with any of the details. Then we can come up with a plan. I don't wanna talk shop in front of Rachel, alright?"

His brow raised at her. "A plan? Alright, I can go with that." He sipped the coffee. "So, how much stuff is Rachel planning to bring?"

"No idea. She can bring anything she wants; I'll make room. I want her there," she said firmly.

Dale smiled. "It's good to see you this happy, Soph."

She glanced at him quickly before putting her eyes back on the road ahead. There wasn't much traffic around, but she wanted to concentrate. "I feel different with her," she said, chancing another glance to make sure that he wasn't laughing at her. His face was open, smiling casually as he sat back and sipped more coffee. "With Yvonne I was always so..."

"Intense, miserable, hard work?" he said, grinning more widely now.

An arched brow shut him up. "Yeah, probably. I prefer focused, dedicated, and hard-working."

They both laughed. She indicated right and waited in the road to take the turn.

"But, seriously. I love her, like, I really love her, and I really want this to work out, more than anything. I'd even give the job up, if she asked me." She took the turning and moved up a gear.

"Fuck, you have got it bad. You'd give up chasing bad guys, late nights, and dealing with morons?" He laughed again. "I dunno, life without Whitton? Wouldn't be the same."

"I didn't say I was going to!" She shook her head, laughing as the little cottage came into view. "Anyway, let's get this done."

~Grave~

Rachel picked up a box and set it down on the table, unpacking it slowly. It hadn't taken long to get the things she wanted to take with her into the van. Dale and Sophie worked like troupers, joking around, barely a complaint from either of them. But now, as Sophie perched on the edge of the sofa drinking a cup of coffee, Rachel wasn't sure what to make of her silence. Every so often she would suck in a deep breath and exhale slowly, deliberately. Her knee bounced rhythmically, and she had that look on her face that said she was contemplating something serious.

"Is everything ok?" Rachel asked when Sophie swallowed down the last of her drink and placed the cup on the coffee table with a gentle chink.

Her dark head whipped around as she forced a smile on her face. "Yeah, course." She stood up and fidgeted with her trousers before crossing the room and peering into the box that Rachel was working through. "Need a hand?"

"If you want to. Where do you want me to put these?" She held up a pair of ornamental figurines, but in reality, she meant the entire box, which contained a few of the new treasures she had been collecting in the months since The Doll Maker.

Sophie's dark eyes captured hers and held them, her brow furrowing. "Anywhere you want to. This isn't my home, and your things." She put down the bubble-wrapped ornament she had picked up. "This is our place, our things. I don't want you to just fit in around me; I want you to overwhelm me with your presence. I want to see you everywhere I look. I want to come home from work, close that door, and leave all that is dark behind me and be wrapped up in you." She stepped forwards and took the figure from Rachel's hand. Linking their fingers, she smiled. "I love you. You light up my world with all that you are, and all these remind me that you're here, you're with me, lighting me up and dragging me out of the darkness."

Rachel all but whimpered as she snaked her arms around Sophie's neck. "Take me to bed."

Sophie grinned, kissing the tip of her nose. "As much as that idea really appeals to me right now, I have to go out and I need a favour."

Rachel pouted. "Where is more important than right here?" She started to undo the buttons on her shirt, putting her ample cleavage on display. Her body was a weapon, armed and primed.

Laughing at her antics, Sophie kissed her quickly. "I promise, I won't be long. I just need to speak with the pathologist."

"You're turning me down for Tristan?"

"I am not turning you down, I am pressing pause and holding that thought." This time when she kissed her, she let it deepen, pressing herself against Rachel's soft flesh. "I won't be long." She removed herself quickly and moved towards the door.

"Fine, what's the favour?" Rachel called out after her.

"Can I borrow the cottage, just for a few days?"

Rachel's eyes narrowed. "Just what are you up to?"

"I just need somewhere out of the way so me and the boys can work in privacy."

Rachel nodded and turned back to the box, but Sophie's words drew her back to her lover.

"Just...bear with me, okay? When I get into work mode and you feel like I'm not here, remind me, don't let me linger in the dark too long." It was the most honest she had ever been with a romantic partner. It felt good to ask Rachel for help and not just bottle it all up like she had with Yvonne.

"Always, Detective. Now, go do your thing, and Sophie?" She smiled seductively and undid another button to her blouse. "Seriously, don't be long. I need some attention."

Heat rose in an instant. Expelling air slowly from her lungs in a deliberate attempt to compose herself, Sophie grinned back. "I won't be long."

Chapter Forty

Tristan Barnard had never been invited anywhere by DI Whitton that didn't involve a crime scene or a pub to celebrate. He was intrigued with the casual offer to pop round to Rachel's for a catch up. So here he was, walking up the pathway of a very quaint-looking cottage with a for sale sign. All was not as it seemed, he considered.

It was even more confusing when DS Saint opened the door and he entered into a room filled with other detectives hard at work on laptops and other screens set up at the dining room table.

"Well, Whitton, I have to say I am a little disappointed. Our first date and all." He took his lightweight jacket off and looked around for somewhere to hang it. Saint took it off him and did the job for him.

"I needed to speak to you away from…well, you'll see. Take a seat." She offered him one of the high-back dining chairs next to Jeff. "We know who our vigilante is."

His eyes widened as he turned to face her. "Okay?" He sounded hesitant. He'd been dragged away from his lab, away from prying eyes and listening ears. He didn't like where this was heading.

"It's Jonas Robinson," she stated and nodded to Jeff. The image of a smart man in his fifties and then stills of the same man wearing a blue boiler suit appeared on the screen. "Here." She pointed to the last image. "This is an internet café in town. He sent me an email from here, and then when he left, he dropped this." She held up an image of the matchbook.

"I know about that, I processed it." He half smiled at her. "What's your evidence that this was him?" he asked, turning away from the screen, not wholly convinced just yet.

She licked her lower lip and reached for a pile of paperwork. He took it when she held it out to him. "Each of these is a related case. Going back years. York, Bristol, Kent and all the surrounding areas. In each case, Jonas worked or lived there."

"But you don't actually have any evidence other than the DNA from the Kent case?"

"Once we get a warrant, I think we will find all the evidence we need. We have a tyre print remember, and the skin cream you found. The problem is, we are talking about a very experienced defence lawyer, and I want to make sure we have this wrapped up so tight that he has no chance to wriggle his way out of it," she explained while her team nodded in unison.

"And we need you to play ball with any potential evidence we might find," Saint chipped in.

Barnard stood up abruptly. "If you're asking me to participate in planting evidence, then the answer is no. That would make us just as bad."

"Chill, Doc." Jeff smiled. "We ain't gonna plant evidence."

"Then what?" He turned back to Whitton and found her grinning.

"I need a scapegoat."

~Grave~

Monday morning brought a downpour. The heavens opened and rain came down in sheets. Whitton ran from her car into the station and was drenched. Running a hand through her hair, she heard a wolf whistle from one of the uniforms as they passed. Looking down, she realised that her shirt was practically see-through. "Terrific," she mumbled to herself. At least she had had the good sense to wear a vest under it.

"Whitton, my office," Turner called out across the room as she walked through the door. "Get a coffee."

Coffee in hand, she knocked on the door and opened it. Her boss looked up at her. The usually calm and put-together detective looked disheveled and out of sorts. He smiled, proffering the chair while he finished up his report.

"Where are we?"

"We have everything linked and yet, nothing concrete that a good defence lawyer couldn't swat away as circumstantial."

"And you're sure it's him?"

"100%."

"I trust you Whitton. I give you far more leeway than I do anyone else. I read your email. Don't fuck this up; if it's him, I want the evidence and I want him put away."

"Yes, sir."

~Grave~

The courts were quiet as Whitton strolled in through security. A quick nod to Tom and then she was perusing the boards. Court One looked her best bet. She took long strides towards the stairs and then climbed them two at a time. When she reached the waiting area, she took a moment to catch her breath and calm herself.

The room was almost empty, just a couple of teenagers in clean hoodies and an older woman looking nervously around her. It was obvious to Whitton's trained eye which ones had been here before and which one was a first timer.

She slipped inside the court room and took a seat at the back, scanning the room quickly to see if

Jonas was there. He wasn't, and she considered briefly whether to try one of the other rooms. She quickly stood and headed towards the door, reaching for the handle, when it opened and in walked the very man she had been hoping to chat to. He smiled at her instantly, and she felt the urge to punch him in the face surge up, but she controlled her reactions and politely returned the smile.

"DI Whitton, what brings you here?" He spoke with such confidence in himself. In another world, Whitton had liked him. He was a good lawyer.

"Actually, I wanted a quick word with you, if you have a moment?"

He checked his watch. "Yes, I can spare a couple of minutes. I'm not due to perform for another half an hour," he confided, leaning in to her as he spoke. "Let me just drop my stuff off." He held up the briefcase in his hand as evidence.

"Great, I'll wait for you outside."

The two teenagers now had a brief with them as they sat looking bored and uninterested in the entire proceedings. She recognised the solicitor and gave an acknowledging nod his way just as the door behind her opened and Jonas stepped out.

"So, what can I do for the best detective in Woodington?" He grinned at her, and now she saw nothing but a smarmy charlatan in front of her. She remembered the email, the arrogance oozing from him.

She looked around and then, touching his elbow, led him to the hallway where nobody could overhear. "The thing is, I was hoping for some advice."

"Of course, go on."

"Okay, this is obviously just between you and me, right?"

He smiled once more. "Of course."

"So, the thing is, we think we made a mistake with Galahad Benson," she admitted, her eyes sinking to the floor in embarrassment.

"Oh, right. In what way?"

"The DNA sample, it's too degraded. Look, I know he is your client, but we both know he did it." She looked him square in the face and noted the flicker of something in his eyes: jubilance. "Of course, you have to defend him anyway. I can't even begin to imagine how you deal with it," she added sympathetically.

Her change of direction threw him for a moment. "Sorry. What?"

She lowered her voice to all but a whisper. "You know, when we all know the fuckers are guilty, but..." She left it unspoken and shrugged, but he got it. "I'm just saying, I know it's probably the shitty part of your job, right?"

"Well, yes, of course. We're not monsters, regardless of how the prosecution paint us." He laughed

"Exactly, I know you're just doing your job. We all know that. It's just a fucking craw in the throat ya know, when we work so hard to catch them and then…"

"I can assure you, Detective, that I take no pleasure in seeing my guilty clients go free; however, the law is what it is. I remember when I first started out, one of the first clients I had was a vicar. A man of God, for Christ sake. Accused of molesting a nun, would you believe that?" He shook his head. "Got off because the jury couldn't accept that a man of God would do such a thing."

"Shocking," Whitton agreed, desperately trying to keep her excitement under the radar. "Anyway, I've taken up too much of your time already. I just wanted you to know that we probably won't be going any further with Benson for now, but we all know the man's guilty, right? It's only a matter of time before we get him."

"Right, well thanks for the heads up. I'm sure he will be relieved."

Chapter Forty-One

As Whitton drove back towards the station, the sun came out from behind the clouds. She reached into her pocket and pulled out her sunglasses, slipping them on over her eyes. Coming to a halt at the lights, she called Saint using the hands-free.

It didn't ring for long before his south London accent boomed into her ears.

"Get on the computer and search through every case Jonas defended that involved a vicar," she ordered.

"Hello to you too," he said sarcastically. "I suppose you have no time frame at all?"

"Nope, just that he mentioned this case in particular. Find it; I want the details ASAP. Something about it could be the trigger."

"Okay, then I will start around '93 then, seeing as that's the first one that we know about."

"Great, I am heading back in now."

"Okay, get us a decent coffee, will ya?"

She disconnected the call and swung the car into the left-hand lane. Something about it all still bothered her, but she couldn't quite put her finger on it. Before she could contemplate it any further, the phone buzzed in its cradle. Whitton smiled as she noted the name and face that flashed up on the screen.

"Hey," she said, smiling still as the cars in front slowed.

"Hello you, I was just wondering if you fancied doing something later?" Rachel's voice was a welcome interruption to the day's events so far.

"Yes, I mean in principle I think that would be nice, unless..."

"Yes, unless Woodington's criminal element need you more than I do." Rachel chuckled to herself, and Whitton thought that it might be the best sound she had heard all day. "Oh, and please do not forget that we have your mother coming over at the weekend, and as much as I like her, I really don't want to spend the day without you there to help keep her entertained.

This time it was Whitton who laughed. "She's not that bad."

"No, she isn't, but she isn't you, and funnily enough, I like spending my days off with you." The traffic lights changed, and Whitton slipped the car into gear, ready to move off again.

"I will do my best to be there while you entertain my mother. You know she likes you more than me," Whitton stated, only half joking.

"Well, that's probably because I don't bugger off halfway through dinner to deal with a murder scene that Dale or Jeff are quite capable of dealing with."

"Ouch, you wound me!" Whitton laughed once more before becoming serious. "But I take your point onboard. I will make sure that someone else is on call Saturday." She smiled. "So long as we don't have a situation with..."

"Hmm, let's hope you wrap that up sooner rather than later," Rachel said before adding, "Comedy or action?"

"Huh?"

"Cinema, tonight, I am booking tickets for the late showing."

"Ah, okay, well whatever you want to watch is fine by me."

With the call ended, something clicked into place within Whitton's mind. She swung the car around the corner and pulled into the parking space outside of the coffee shop. She grabbed coffees and pastries and then headed back to the station to check out her theory.

~Grave~

Dale had his hand out the moment he spotted her entering the room.

"Oh, how I need you," he said to the red paper cup that she held out to him. He took it, flicking the top off, and took a gulp of the now-drinkable coffee. "God, that's like nectar."

"Glad to be of service. What did you find?"

Dale sat back in his seat and grimaced. "Bugger all, really." He picked up his pad and read out the details. "Vicar got away with it, that's all true. But he is still alive and well up in Northampton. The court case took place in 1992. So, before the first grave murder – that we know of."

"Damn, I was hoping that would be the connection." She perched on the edge of his desk and took a sip of her own drink. "I had another thought, but..."

Intrigued, he sat forward. "Go on."

"Well it was just, he was raised by an aunt, not his mother, right?"

"The mother's sister took him in cos the father was at sea."

"Where are either of them?"

He swiveled his chair around to face the desk and started typing. "Okay, here we go. Petty Officer James Robinson." His eyes scanned the page further. "Shit."

"What?" She stood and leaned in over his shoulder.

"Name: PO J ROBINSON

Date of Death: 3rd February 1993

Cause of Death: Accidental Drowning.

Factors: On the night of 3rd Feb, PO Robinson and CPO Hansen were both intoxicated. They got into a fight and PO Robinson fell overboard. The alarm was raised and a search of the harbour took place, however, PO Robinson's body was not found until the following day.

It was recommended that CPO Hansen be demoted to PO for his part in the altercation. No further action was taken."

"Where is this Hansen?"

Dale's fingers moved swiftly over the keys as he typed in the information. When it appeared on the screen, he sat back and ran his hands over his face. "Dead, accidental drowning."

"Accidental?"

"Just what I was thinking." He sighed. "This could have been his trigger. If he took revenge, meted out his own form of justice..."

"The graves aspect could have come later."

Chapter Forty-Two

At eight a.m. there was barely a sign of life within Mutare. Jonas Robinson had been there on many an occasion, but never this early before. He'd found a certain calmness that came from his visits. The meditations and the easygoing way that Jewel and Galahad managed the different people and issues was, in his opinion, nothing short of magnificent. It was a shame really that it had to come to an end, but he knew that this was a gilt-edged opportunity that he couldn't let pass.

He pulled his car into the space right outside of the property and sat in his seat for a moment, composing himself. This would be different. Before he had always had right on his side, a sense of justice pushing him forward to complete the necessary actions in order to realign the universal righteousness.

Not once had he ever delivered a blow that wasn't justified and righteous. This would be a little different, but the end justified the means. They were too close. Whitton wasn't an idiot, and she wouldn't let this go, not unless the case was closed. He could close the case for her.

Climbing from the car, he stretched his spine as he hit the lock button. The garden was in need of some attention, he noted as he strolled up the path and banged gently on the door. It didn't take long to hear the sounds of life inside.

When Jewel opened the door, he smiled pleasantly at her.

"Jonas, what a surprise, come in." She smiled and stepped aside for him. The remnants of incense burned hours ago still wafted through the house. He liked the smell.

"I was just wondering if Galahad was around. I have a few loose ends to tie up with him," he said, following her into the kitchen.

She lifted the kettle. "Tea?"

"Oh, no thanks. I just wanted a quick word, really."

She filled the kettle and put it back on the base that would boil the water. "I'm afraid I just don't know what to do. He's…" She ran her hand through her hair and sighed. "I think our marriage is falling apart and he's…I think he has someone else."

"Ah, that's…" He remembered his client's admission and considered whether he should divulge anything to this poor woman, but that wouldn't help his own cause. "Is he here?"

She shook her head, tears forming. "No, I think he is with her. I followed him yesterday. I know I shouldn't have, but…"

"Where did he go?"

Pulling a piece of paper out from under the bread bin, she slid it across to him and let him read the address. It was not too far away, just on outskirts of Woodington.

"What do you think I should do?"

"I...well, I think that you should probably confront him. It isn't going to be easy, but honesty is surely the best policy. Isn't that what we learn at Mutare?"

She smiled and pulled the paper away, pushing it back under the bread bin. "You're right."

Reaching out a hand, he ran it sympathetically down her arm before turning towards the door. "Okay, well I will be off then. If you do see him, please ask him to call me."

She followed him out and waved when he turned back at the gate. The sun in her eyes, she squinted as he climbed into his car and felt for the phone in her pocket, only pulling it out once he had driven away and was out of sight.

"Hello, yes...he knows."

Chapter Forty-Three

He loosened his tie. Sitting inside the car without the engine running meant that it was stifling. The boiler suit only added to the heat. He considered letting the engine run for a while so that the air conditioning could cool everything down, but he didn't wasn't to draw any attention to himself. Instead, he wiped his face with a hankie and kept a close eye on the small cottage.

The for-sale sign looked new. The grass was cut and the beds flowering, tall sunflowers enjoying the heat that poured upon them. They straightened and pushed their faces towards it.

It was a quiet road, for which he was grateful, and so far, he had seen nobody pass him by. He pulled the cap down lower, just in case. He had seen only the woman; a tall blonde with ample bosom had come in laden with shopping bags an hour before. Galahad had opened the door and smiled, greeting her with a kiss and a furtive look up and down the road as she passed by him and into the cottage.

That was the moment when Jonas finally justified in his own mind what it was he was about to do. Until now, he had seen Galahad as the innocent patsy, the man caught in the web who would be the key to Jonas' own freedom. Now though, he saw him for what he was: a cheat. Jewel was nothing but a supportive and exceptional wife to him and a mentor to those who were victims in this world. She deserved better than this fool.

Wiping his face for the umpteenth time, his attention was caught. There was movement at the door again. This time, the woman was leaving. She reached up and wrapped her hands around his neck, and they held each other as she whispered something to him. He smiled and pulled back to look at her before inching forward to kiss her lips quickly. She waved as she turned and walked back down the path, waving again at the gate before marching confidently off down the street, turning right at the corner. Galahad closed the door behind him, and Jonas stepped out of the car.

Carrying his small bag, he looked like any plumber or handyman who might be working. He strolled up the path and knocked on the door, only glancing around once, finding the street empty. He smiled to himself. Luck was always on his side.

The door swung open. "What did you forget?" Galahad laughed and then frowned as he took in the man standing before him. "Jonas?"

"Galahad, can I come in?" He took one more furtive glance around. Still nobody on the street, but he would rather not hang around outside when he had so much to do.

Stepping aside, Galahad said, "Of course," his eyes narrowing a little as he tried to work out why his friend wasn't wearing the customary suit. "How did you know where to find me?"

Jonas smiled. "Oh you know how it is, ~~us~~ WE law enforcement types can usually find someone when we need to." He lied with such ease that he almost believed it himself. "I am sorry to turn up unannounced, but it is important that I see you. Am I keeping you from anything?"

Leading the way into the living room, Galahad shook his head. "No, June...she uh, she's my friend, the one I told you about at the station. She's just bought this place and..." He had the decency to blush at least, Jonas considered. The world of mistresses and deceit was a murky one after all, and didn't it deserve a little embarrassment? "Anyway, she has gone into town for more cleaning products. Moving in officially tomorrow with all of her boxes of knickknacks." His eyes followed Jonas as both men surveyed the nearly empty room. An old sofa and a table with four chairs were pretty much all that was there. "So, tea? I think there is a pint of milk now."

Smiling, Jonas nodded. "Why not?"

The kitchen was just a small room off of the living room. Nowhere to go. Jonas watched as Galahad filled the kettle and flicked the switch to boil. Opening his bag, he pulled out the syringe and took the protective cap off as two cups chinked together when Galahad pulled them from the cupboard. "So, what was it that you wanted to tell me?"

Thoughtfully, Jonas considered the question before deciding honesty was the best policy as always. He stepped up behind the big man. "I wanted to apologise," he said as he plunged the needle into Galahad's neck, pressing the plunger instantly. "Because, I have to kill you," he continued, catching Galahad's weight as he slumped. "Don't worry, I'll make yours as painless as I can."

Galahad clawed up at him with a meaty fist, but Jonas managed to dodge to the side, dropping him gently to the floor.

"See, the thing is G, the police need an answer and right now, you're their best bet. And I have far too much to do keeping the guilty off of the streets and the innocents out of jail. So, you see, it's really just..." He grabbed Galahad under the arms and pulled him into the living area. Dragging him along the old carpet, he considered the fibers that would be collecting on the material. Any decent ME worth their salt would work out in an instant that he hadn't got into the chair without help. Lifting a dead weight onto the sofa was hard work. Undressing him and leaving him in nothing but his underpants was even more difficult.

Galahad's eyes locked on him as he fought to focus. "Don't worry, I've given you a good dose of ketamine. Not enough to kill you, just...well, I need you pliable, G. Got to make it look like it all became too much for you and well, what with the police about to arrest you any minute...who would blame you if you did take the easy way out, huh?"

There was a grunt from the prone man, followed by a slurred, "Why?"

"Are you asking why I play judge and executioner?" There was a small nod, and Jonas smiled sadly. "I suppose you do deserve an explanation." He crossed the room again quickly and picked up his bag, bringing it over to where Galahad was now lying as though he were going to take a nap. "Well, I guess I was quite young when I first realised that justice didn't mean the same to everyone. My mother died when I suppose I needed her most, and though my aunt did as best a job as she could, it wasn't the same." He pulled out another syringe and began to fill it with something clear from a small bottle. "And then, as though that wasn't enough, my father was killed in an *accident*." He flicked the syringe and pushed the air bubble out. "But really, I think it was the Grayson case that did it for me. I'd watched so many clients get off with technicalities and inept prosecution briefs that it was like a pressure cooker."

He noticed Galahad's eyes begin to close. The ketamine working perfectly to knock the big man out long enough to finish the job. As he talked, however, he found it a little cathartic. This would be the end of it; in reality, he couldn't continue after this. Pouring out his confession to the man who would take the blame felt only fair.

"Grayson was a horrible little man. The kind of man that you took one look at and wanted so slap him because you already knew he was up to no good. Repeatedly, he would come before the courts, and every time there would be some reason why he wouldn't be given a custodial sentence. And remember, these were only the crimes he had been caught for; there were many more where he hadn't."

He perched himself on the edge of the sofa. "I know what you're thinking," he chuckled. "What grisly crime, who did he murder? It wasn't that. He was a petty criminal really, but it all adds up, doesn't it? Every little fraud, scam, theft. All of those people whose lives are affected because this horrible piece of shit could get away with it." Gently he lifted Galahad's right eyelid. "Hmm, Mabel Grimes saved all of her life to enjoy a small pension and live a modest, but comfortable last few years – funnily enough, in a cottage just like this...only he took it all away, in a driveway scam. Every last penny she had, he took it. He actually got sent down for it: six months, out in three. Mabel Grimes died two months after he was sentenced. Had a stroke, from the stress of it all I imagine."

He exhaled loudly and stood back up. "I was in a pub not that long after, and he was there with some of his cronies, and he had the audacity to thank Mabel as he handed over a £20 note to pay for his drinks. So I killed him, left him in the back alley by the bins, best place for him. But after that, I thought of poor Mabel and I wished I could have let her know that it was all okay now. That he had got what he deserved. That was when I came up with the idea to leave them with their victim. Just letting them know that justice had been served." He wiped gently at the crease of the elbow of Galahad's right arm. "Anyway, I'll make this quick. And I'll keep an eye on Jewel, make sure that she doesn't find out about this..." He looked around the room. "...little arrangement...though, I can't guarantee that the police won't blab it."

A rush of noise came all at once: footsteps charging down the stairs, the front door crashing open, and voices screaming at him.

"Police!"

"Move away from the sofa."

"Back away now. On the floor."

It was all a cacophony of sound as Jonas tried to stand, the needle still in his hand. He looked up and saw the face of Whitton as she organised medical personnel to deal with Galahad. His patsy was coming around. It would be a while before he was completely compos mentis, but he would be okay.

As his eyes locked with Whitton's, he smiled. Luck had been good to him; now though, it had run out. Maybe his time had run out too. He didn't feel the prick, or the rush of liquid as it entered his bloodstream. He just kept his eyes on her as very quickly his vision blurred, his focus went sleepy, and then she was gone.

He could still hear the voices, the scream from Whitton to stop him, but it was too late. Nothing could save him now.

It was ironic, fitting in a way, that he be his own judge and executioner.

Epilogue

Whitton lounged on the couch with her feet up on the table as Rachel pottered around the kitchen making tea for them all. Sophie's mother had arrived late the previous night, and this was the first real opportunity they had had to speak.

"I can't believe that you used Rachel's dear little cottage to capture your prey," Gaynor Whitton said with a wry smile of her face. She knew all too well that her daughter would always do whatever it took to catch her man.

"It wasn't like I didn't ask for permission first," Sophie argued, looking up to catch the raised brow of her lover as she worked at the counter. "Okay, so I didn't quite explain my plan, but to be fair, I hadn't actually worked it all out at that point."

"True, you got lucky there," her mother agreed quickly, receiving a glare in return.

"It all worked out just as we planned, in the end. Turner wasn't happy about using Galahad, but he'd agreed to it. Seems he really has reformed. He wasn't happy about being the patsy for Jonas' crimes. But yeah, we got lucky. I'm not sure Galahad would have been quite so eager to help if he had known about the ketamine in advance," she admitted with a crooked grin on her face. "Jonas though, he thought he was going to be his own executioner. But the paramedics put a stop to that. He volunteered a confession again at the station. We got it all on tape and video. The CPS are going to throw the book at him." She stood and moved across the room to the fan, hitting the oscillation button so the cold air would penetrate the entire room.

"Once he is out of hospital," Rachel added from across the room, watching Sophie as she moved about before she finally sat back down in the same spot.

"Yes, but he will make a full recovery, and then he will finally stand trial for his crimes," Whitton answered, a determined edge to her voice.

Gaynor fidgeted and got comfortable, sitting exactly the same way that her daughter did. In so many ways they were alike. Rachel knew where Sophie's strong personality came from, as well as her dark, brooding looks.

"It's a shame really, I mean, if he hadn't been so wrong with, Anita Simmons, was it?" Whitton nodded at her mother. "Then most likely he would have gained public sympathy. A lot of people would consider what he did as a good deed."

"That's why we have police officer's mother, and anyway, he didn't mind getting paid to defend these people. He isn't some angel that spared the world. He is a murderer who calculatingly took the lives of people he deemed guilty. Anita Simmons' husband and two daughters are the victims of that; they're the ones who deserve sympathy."

"I suppose you are right."

Rachel brought the tray over and placed a mug of coffee in front of each of them. Sophie reached for the Wonder Woman cup and sipped gingerly while her mother turned to Rachel. "And how are things with you now?" she asked, the implication of that question being more than just 'how is work these days.'

Taking a seat next to Sophie, she felt her hand being taken and watched as Sophie raised it to her lips and kissed the back of it. She smiled and felt herself melt into the warmth of her lover. "I think I am doing a lot better now. We had some dark days to get through, but I think we're on the other side now, and things are looking pretty good from where I am sitting."

"I do worry about you both." Gaynor smiled sadly. "It's such a traumatic experience that you both went through, I just..."

"No," Sophie said instantly. "No, you are not." Her head shook, black hair swinging in front of her eyes. "Mother, we are quite fine as we are. I have Dr. Westbrook if I need her, and Rachel is going to be seeing someone. We do not need you to move here."

"I wasn't going..."

"Yes, you were. I know that face." Sophie grinned at her mother as Rachel looked back and forth between them.

"Fine, I was." She laughed. "But only because I miss seeing you. We could, what is it you call it, hang out?"

"Dear God, you would hate it here, Mum. Stay by the sea where you can feed the gulls and we can visit."

Rachel chipped in, "It is nice having somewhere on the coast to go for a holiday." She pulled her feet up and tucked them to the side as she leant against Sophie a little more, enjoying the feeling of her arm as it snaked around her waist. "I promise, I will make her take time off and we will visit more often."

"Actually, I was thinking maybe somewhere a bit further afield." Sophie smiled and reached down to the side table. Lifting a magazine, she pulled a leaflet out from under it. "I was in town and popped into the travel agents. They had a great deal on for a break in Turkey."

Twisting in her seat, Rachel's eyes lit up. "You booked us a holiday?"

"I did. I mean, Becky spoke to the powers that be, and they said if you got a form in on Monday to book the leave, you'd get it."

"When do we go?"

"A week, Wednesday. For two weeks."

Rachel suddenly stopped smiling, "You said the other day that you were sick of the heat."

"I said I was sick of working in this heat, not swimming in a pool and drinking Mojitos," Whitton insisted. "Plus, you do keep wearing that bikini, so I figure I might as well take you somewhere to really show it off."

As Rachel read through the brochure, Whitton's phone buzzed in her pocket. Reaching in, she pulled it free and saw the number, groaning. "Whitton."

"Guv, there's been an incident..." The serious voice of Coleen O'Leary spoke eloquently down the phone. Whitton eyed the room, her mother watching closely. Rachel quietly stiffened.

"I see." Her old self would already be dislodging Rachel and standing, ready to leave. But something stopped her this time. She'd been making grave decisions her entire working career; now it was time to make some brave decisions. "Call Jeff. I'll get a rundown on Monday." She ended the call and felt Rachel relax and settle against her again. This was what she needed now.

Work could wait.

If you enjoyed this book, or any other of Claire's books, then please consider leaving a review.
Many thanks!
UK Readers
https://amzn.to/2QNNd5E
US Readers
https://amzn.to/2XCes4J
French Readers
https://amzn.to/2XzPgMg
German Readers
https://amzn.to/2KKUyiO
Australian Readers
https://amzn.to/34bbzuh

If you want to know more about Claire, you can follow her on Social media.
Facebook: https://www.facebook.com/ItsClaStevWriter/
Twitter: https://twitter.com/ClaStevOfficial
Instagram: https://www.instagram.com/itsclastevofficial/
Tumblr: https://www.tumblr.com/blog/itsclastevofficial
Blog: https://wordpress.com/view/itsclastevofficialblog.com
Website: http://www.itsclastevofficial.co.uk

For the chance to win prizes, get exclusive updates on new releases, free stories, and much more, why not sign up to Claire's monthly newsletter?
Subscribe here: http://bit.ly/2D9BiXS

Two women escaping their own demons. One stuck in the past, the other a very real present.

Lucy Owens' life was irrevocably changed in a matter of seconds. Life as she knew it was over in the blink of an eye. Moving away from all that she knew, Lucy now lives a solitary life in her cabin on the shores of Lake Tahoe. Filled with guilt and pain, she keeps herself to herself, and for years she manages to avoid immersing back into society. Nicole Granger has three small children to worry about. Always looking over her shoulder, they arrive at the lake with very little to call their own. Haunted by years of physical abuse, she longs to belong again, to bring normality to her girls' lives for the first time.

Both women are pulled towards one another in an attraction that could bring both of them their freedom.
http://getbook.at/Escapeandfreedom

Brooke Chambers is forced to leave the Army and the job that she loves. Moving back into civilian life, she never imagined it would mean looking after her teenage sister and searching for a new career.

But, with the sudden loss of their dad, Brooke finds herself stepping up, and in the process, looking for a new job; any job.

Getting the chance to let off some steam, she heads to Art, a lesbian bar, and meets Catherine. It's lust at first sight as both women feel that instant connection, despite the obvious age gap.

With Brooke's new job being the same place where Catherine works, she assumes it was meant to be. Catherine, however, has other ideas and puts a halt to any prospective love affair, much to Brooke's confusion and heartbreak.

When she tells Brooke to forget it, she didn't quite mean it so literally and wishes she hadn't said it, but Brooke is injured on the job and loses her memory...and forgets Catherine....

Will they get a second chance to work things out?

http://getbook.at/ForgetITCHS

Ren Dyer is at the pinnacle of her career. Newly appointed as head of the protection team for Home Secretary Andrea Fielding, she is a woman focused only on her job.

Andrea Fielding is a woman who is looking for love and finding it in all the wrong places.

When the worst happens and the world changes dramatically around them, will Andrea finally see what's been right in front of her all along?

On the road, together with a group of people that includes Andrea's ex, Dutch Foreign Minister Marja Stegenga, they must try to reach the safety of HQ at the other end of the country.

For Ren Dyer, it is simple: keep her safe.

For Andrea Fielding, it's anything but...

As protocols shift and rules go out the window, will Ren see there is more to life than work, and will Andrea finally find the love she is searching for?

http://viewbook.at/InDyerNeed

Printed in Great Britain
by Amazon